Sting in the Tail

Sting in the Tail

Gerald Hammond

St. Martin's Press
New York

M

Library of Congress Cataloging-in-Publication Data

Hammond, Gerald
    Sting in the tail / Gerald Hammond.
       p.   cm.
    ISBN 0-312-13189-5
    1. Cunningham, John (Fictitious character)—Fiction.   2. Dog—breeders—Scotland—Highlands—Fiction.   3. Highlands (Scotland)—Fiction.   I. Title.
PR6058.A55456S67   1995
823'.914—dc20   95-14717
                                                CIP

First published in Great Britain by Macmillan London Limited

First U.S. Edition: August 1995
10 9 8 7 6 5 4 3 2 1

AUTHOR'S NOTE

At the time of writing (1993), the law and other constraints surrounding both setaside land and tail docking were as stated in the text. The rules of setaside have since been modified.

It is difficult to believe that our legislators and the governing body of veterinary surgeons will continue, let alone succeed, in their efforts to prevent the docking of the tails of working gundogs – a practice which is carried out with good reason and in the interests of the dogs themselves.

G.H.

ONE

I was supposed – by my partners – to be catching up on such news in the various sporting magazines as might be of professional interest to us. But, not for the first time, a day spent in the cold, fresh air, teaching a succession of spaniels the essence of their future jobs, had caught up with me and I had dozed off in front of the sitting-room fire. My wife's arrival jerked me back into the waking world.

I snatched a quick glance towards our son, over whom I was supposed to be keeping a watchful eye, but Sam, in his playpen, had also dozed off. He had been chewing on a woollen elephant. I had only been chewing on a problem.

I accepted Beth's apologies awkwardly. I was almost recovered now from the illness that had ended my army career, but I had given them several frights along the way and Beth, in common with my other partner Isobel, persisted in treating me as if I were a piece of fragile china. This I found mildly comforting when I was off colour and a humiliating nuisance when I was not. So while I felt guilty for sleeping, Beth felt guilty for waking me up. In the midst of so much guilt, love grew like a weed.

'I'll leave you to have the other twenty winks,' she said softly.

'I'm awake,' I told her.

'Sleep if you want to. It's dark outside and the work's all done.' She paused doubtfully, but when I shook my head she came all the way into the room, stooped to add a couple of logs to a fire which had almost expired and then sat down beside me. 'It's about tomorrow. Nothing to worry about,' she added quickly in case I should worry myself into a relapse. 'But one of the Guns has broken his wrist and cried off.'

I cast my mind back. 'It's the same party that came at the end of October, isn't it?' I asked. 'From Edinburgh?'

'That's right.'

'Which one's injured?'

'Mr Sangster,' Beth said. 'He's the tall man with the ginger moustache.'

'And a retriever to match. I remember him. Damn it!' I added. 'He's the only one of that bunch that can shoot. They'd booked for a hundred-bird day?'

'A hundred and fifty, this time,' Beth said. 'They seem to have enjoyed themselves.'

'They'll never make it without him. They'll blow off a thousand rounds, bring down fifty birds and try to get off with paying accordingly. We have Mr Sangster's deposit safe and sound?'

'Of course.'

I gave it some more thought. Our business was a breeding and training kennel, primarily of working springer spaniels although with occasional excursions. But any trainer of working gundogs, especially if he aspires to success in field trials and the kudos and prices that that success brings, needs ready access to ground with at least a modicum of game, so we had gone into partnership with Angus Todd to run a commercial shoot.

Privately I had mixed feelings about operating a commercial shoot and providing sport for busy executives or facilities for them to entertain their most important associates, all at so much per bird. I had been brought up to believe that one paid for one's shooting, not just with money but with service to the land. On the other hand, it was a reasonable money-spinner, a valuable training facility and an equally valuable shop window for the dogs. If the visitors were prepared to delegate to us their share of service to the land and to pay accordingly, so much the better.

Angus attended to most of the keepering while, by combining visits to his snares and feeders with our usual training sessions, we helped out whenever he was busy rearing pheasant poults for the shoot and for sale, or when he was conducting visiting parties in pursuit of wild geese. As a keeper, Angus was good; but he had no head for management and on shooting days he limited his participation to controlling the line of beaters. The rest was up to us.

'So what will we do?' Beth asked.

Several local men would be happy to fill the gap. I passed them in mental review and made the obvious choice. 'Give Charlie Hopewell a ring,' I said. 'If he's free, he can have the day on the usual terms.' In addition to being a first-class shot who could be counted on to fill the bag – an important consideration on a commercial shoot at which the basis of agreement was a price per bird in the bag – he was always willing to pay up at half the going rate which, taken together with the forfeited deposit, would make up most of the shortfall.

'He'll want to bring that damned dog of his,' Beth said. She rarely indulges in even such modest swearing but I could see her point. Charlie Hopewell had saddled himself with a springer spaniel of excellent pedigree but show-bench lineage. Show springers often lack enough sense to answer to their own names, but Clarence was not quite so low in the batting average as that. He was an affectionate and singularly handsome liver and white springer with good markings and beautifully feathered legs and tail. He even showed a faint vestige of talent. Any dog can crash through the bushes scaring up game, but Clarence, although an exuberant and extroverted dog, was usually controllable and had learned to retrieve after a fashion. On occasions, however, he had been known to run riot.

'I'll make it clear that if Clarence comes he stays on a heavy chain.'

3

'Henry was probably hoping to be asked,' Beth said gently.

Henry was the husband of Isobel, my other partner. He would have expected his day of driven pheasant shooting for nothing, on top of which he might well have got boozed up at lunchtime and missed everything all afternoon.

'Tell Henry we can't spare him from his duties as a host,' I said. Although Henry was not properly a part of the firm, he was a useful standby in times of trouble and always available to meet the guest Guns and entertain them at table. 'Tell him that he can shoot if another Gun cries off.'

'You tell him,' Beth said.

'I'll tell Isobel.'

'All right.' Having reached a satisfactory compromise which did not necessitate either of us having to disappoint Henry, Beth changed tacks. 'Mrs Todd can come over to look after Sam, feed the puppies and keep an eye on the place. Do you want me to pick up with Jason as usual?' Jason was Beth's personal Labrador.

'Of course,' I said.

'Which spaniels are we taking?'

We settled down to the usual lengthy debate. A shooting day with the picking-up and beating under our control was a perfect chance to put a polish on the trained dogs and to sharpen up those with important competitions still to come but, even with frequent exchanges of dogs, there was a limit to the number who could be given experience on a guest day by Isobel and myself. Beth, who would have been perfectly capable of sharing in the advanced training of our stock, was terrified of doing more harm than good, so she limited herself to basic puppy-training – plus, of course, all the duties of wife and mother and gardener.

To add to our burdens, we were once again between kennel-maids, the eccentric Daffy, who had filled the post very satisfactorily for more than a year, having suddenly decided to return to her respectable suburban home. That duty, which had originally brought Beth to Three Oaks Kennels, was hers again for the moment. Somehow, she always managed to cope, with so little complaint that I had to remind myself to be duly grateful and to help out whenever I could.

The morning was fair, or as fair as one has any right to expect in north-east Fife in early December. An overnight frost had lifted and now a thin sun was shining through the low mist that clung to the ground.

A breeze was developing out of the morning's calm and I hoped that there was no real wind to follow. We were developing the shoot to provide difficult birds, a fact which was appreciated by most of our visitors. But any wind above a moderate breeze would put the birds beyond the skill of this particular party; and if they did not enjoy themselves they would neither return nor spread the good word.

Isobel Kitts, the third partner, walked in while we were at breakfast. Beth was spooning something sloshy into Sam, who was sitting up in his high chair and looking very pleased with himself. Although younger than Henry, Isobel was nevertheless a lady of a certain maturity; but she was always on hand when there was work to be done – unless, that is, she had been celebrating the night before. I was relieved to see that she was fresh and alert that morning. For all her motherly appearance and usual comparative sobriety, Isobel could occasionally fall right off the wagon. Henry, she said, had left early to breakfast with the guests.

Beth and I had put in an hour before breakfast, so that little remained to be done. Beth did most of what there was while I went over the order of the day with Isobel. When Angus Todd's Land Rover rattled up the drive and deposited Mrs Todd, the dogs were already in their travelling boxes. Three dogs went into the back of the Land Rover, the others into our old estate car.

We lingered for a few minutes while Beth gave Mrs Todd last-minute instructions about Sam's diet and regime, then got under way. We crossed the Tay by the road bridge, battled through the usual Saturday shopping traffic and left Dundee on the road towards Perth. Some miles later we turned north off the dual carriageway, away from the Tay and under a great skein of greylag geese which were heading for their feeding grounds. After a few miles of country road we came to Foleyburn village and forked right. The Sidlaw Hills began a mile ahead and our destination lay just beyond the first crest. We entered an unpretentious driveway of Foleyknowe and passed the 'big house' which was standing empty.

Angus must have pushed his old Land Rover hard, because we barely managed to arrive at Foleyknowe on his heels.

Thanks to a monetary arrangement with the farmer, an acre of stubble was left unploughed for us until February. Here the beaters and their dogs were already assembling, a mixed crew of men, and two ladies, who turned out week after week just for the fun of it and for the sake of the traditional Keeper's Day at the end of the season. The pay traditionally accorded to beaters would, in any other field, have brought the unions down on the employer's head. Not that many of the team had much need of the money. I recognized several spaniels which we had sold, full or part trained, for substantial sums, and it was not unknown for the better dressed beaters to be smarter than the scruffier Guns. There was a holiday air which communicated itself to the dogs.

By the time Henry and the Guns rolled up in two Range Rovers plus Henry's hatchback, I had had a word with Angus, the beaters were apprised of the outline plan for the day and the first trio of our dogs had been brought out. Joe Little, a neighbouring Labrador trainer who was glad of the extra outing for his dogs, arrived by Volvo to help with the picking-up. Henry's gun in its leather case was prominent on the back seat of his car. I shook my head at him and he shrugged.

Charlie Hopewell, I noticed, arrived in Henry's car, so I guessed that he had joined the others for a hotel breakfast. His spaniel, Clarence, was subdued for once and stayed tight, leaning against Charlie's leg instead of bouncing around and offering himself for patting or making advances to any other canine which he deemed, rightly or wrongly, to be female. Something else was different about him, but I was too busy to think about it.

Isobel went round collecting cheques from those of the Guns who had so far only put down deposits, and then joined the beaters. By long-standing arrangement, Isobel would give the dogs experience of hunting in the line of beaters while I would give retrieving practice by picking up behind the Guns.

Angus and the beaters climbed into the trailer which would convey them to the start of the first drive, while I delivered the usual lecture about good behaviour, safe shooting, keeping dogs under control and trying to mark down any pricked birds. The Guns had heard it before from me, but they listened patiently. They knew that I would have said the same if the party had consisted of Privy Counsellors with a couple of archbishops in attendance.

I led the Guns and dog-handlers away. Henry, driving Angus's Land Rover as game-cart, gave lifts to any Guns who so wished, although the distances involved hardly justified transport. From where we had parked, two valleys, or a single valley with a bend in the middle, ran roughly east and north-west. Dense cover, between fences and hedges, flanked the burns that wandered along the middle of each valley bottom, but at most points there was room for a good-sized and almost level field between the fence and the foot of the nearby hill.

We seldom put out pegs, preferring to stay flexible in case of a sudden change of wind or weather. Usually, I placed the Guns near the foot of the hill so that the pheasants, which had followed strips of game cover to feeders among more cover on the hilltops, would be heading downhill for home, high and very fast, as they passed

7

overhead. But that was not for this party. I lined them out closer to the trees where the birds would be approaching home base. Beth and Joe and I retired among the trees.

A word with Angus over our radios and we heard the beaters begin to work through the bushes on the hilltop. I gave a small sigh of satisfaction. Giving my life over to the training of working dogs was a pleasant way of opting out. But here, in the field, was the sharp end of it all. A primitive joy it might be and far from logical, recovering the poultry which had been released some months before to grow on in the wild and then making it as difficult as the participants could cope with; but it satisfied the inner man. To crown it, our guests were allowed to work their own dogs only on sufferance when given permission and were paying handsomely for the privilege of being ordered about and exposing themselves to the humiliation of missing abominably. I, on the other hand, was free to concentrate on the dog-work – which, as far as I was concerned, was much more fun than shooting – and, what was more, being paid for it.

The birds were coming. Angus had tight control of the beating line and instead of one great flush and a hectic minute or two the pheasants were taking off in a steady trickle, climbing away from the beaters' dogs, then powering and finally gliding downwards, looking deceptively slow until they grew suddenly in size, flicked past high overhead and were gone.

At that spot, I could not get as far back as I would have preferred and still assess the ability of the visitors, so I took up a safe position behind a stout tree. The Gun in front of me, some fifty paces away, was a ditherer. I remembered him from his previous visit. His name, I thought, was Larrowby or something very like it. Bird after bird came for him, well within range and beginning to slow. Each time, he mounted his gun before the bird had come into range, tracked it, hesitated too long and lost sight of it behind. When at last he did get one shot off, he took tail feathers out of a hen pheasant which flew on unhurt. Well, I thought, at least he would not go home with clean barrels. A cock was coming, brilliant in the cold sunshine. He mounted his gun and even from where I stood I could see that he was nicely ahead of it.

'Now!' I roared.

Out of sheer surprise he squawked and pulled a trigger. The cock pheasant's head went back. It turned over, tumbled and bounced, stone-dead, at his feet. It was a shot that almost any man would have relished.

The beaters appeared on the skyline and I sounded a double whistle for the end of the drive. One last bird came over, unsaluted, and we began the pick-up. There were no runners and I soon had all the birds accounted for. A shy figure, blinking with pleasure, had an open and empty gun over one arm and a cock pheasant cradled in the other.

'Nice one!' I said.

He beamed. 'I don't get the chance to shoot very often, Mr Cunningham,' he said. 'I have a shop and Saturday's our busiest day. We have to compete with the Pakistanis.' It was a sort of apology.

I took the bird. He parted with it reluctantly and I made a mental note to ensure that it was included in his brace at close of play. 'That one bird made my day,' he said. 'I'll always remember it. Even if I don't let off another shot today.' Which, I thought, was quite possible.

Lunch had, as usual, been bespoken from the hotel in the nearby village, where any Guns visiting from afar were usually put up. It was served buffet-style from tables set up in a barn. Cold meals prepared and delivered in the morning were supplemented by soup, coffee and hot sausage rolls supplied in insulated containers at midday. That may sound spartan, but the hotel was noted for its cuisine and we had never had any complaints. On an adjoining table a free bar was set out; indeed, the bar was available throughout the day from a hamper in the game-cart, with

9

the proviso, made clear in the preliminary letters, that anyone becoming, in my sole judgement, incapable of responsible gun-handling would be sent to sit in one of the cars. No refunds were ever given.

At the end of the day, the rules were relaxed, but hope sprang eternal in the breast of the local police sergeant, a man of much energy but no vision, that we would one day fall foul of the breathalyser laws. We made sure that anyone beyond the breathalyser limit was chauffeured to his home or hotel by one of us and that all legal requirements, even that of Game Licences, were strictly observed.

The company in the barn was cheerful and relaxed, savouring the morning and looking forward to the afternoon. Mr Larrowby, my friend of the first drive, had been so inspired by his success that he had shot in a manner which was, by his standard, brilliant. The group was more than halfway to its target bag. I had a word with Angus, who with the beaters was enjoying the same lunch but a less lavish bar in the adjoining cart-shed, to warn him against sending over too many easy birds.

Then I sought out Charlie Hopewell. The other Guns knew each other well and had coalesced into a tight group and, although they had not cold-shouldered Charlie, I found him sitting on a straw bale, enjoying the smoked salmon sandwiches and chatting to Beth. Charlie was a small but well-built man in his fifties, open of face and manner. He had straight sandy hair, thinning, over a face that seemed to have run rather to nose, leaving little room for his bushy moustache. He had operated a barely successful architectural practice in Glenrothes and organized very successfully the alterations at Three Oaks when I first bought it. Shortly thereafter he had sold the practice and taken early retirement. A few days after the deal was signed, a former client of Charlie's had walked in with another and far larger commission and the practice had begun to boom at last. But Charlie was not bitter. He had achieved leisure at an earlier age than most men can manage and, unlike many another, he was enjoying it.

We had almost lost touch when Charlie moved to Foley-burn village, but we had picked up the threads again. He was a naturally happy man but with two regrets. One was that his wife had not lived to enjoy retirement with him. The other was that, in dying, she had left him to cope alone with a daughter. Perhaps the girl, Hannah, needed a mother. On the few occasions that I had met her she had seemed well behaved but, although Charlie was understandably reticent on the subject, she was said to be unruly. I knew that his son, older and now married, lived nearby and that the young couple tried to help with Hannah, but the responsibility was Charlie's. All the same, he seemed contented enough, and although his income was now more limited it had made a partial re-covery since Hannah had made herself unwelcome at the latest of a long series of boarding schools. Charlie showed a remarkable knack of finding cheap or free opportunities to shoot or fish.

'Take it easy this afternoon,' I told him. 'I'll keep you advised how many we're still looking for and on the last drive I'll be standing at your elbow. They're paying for a hundred and fifty and that's what they'll get, give or take very few.'

He winked. 'I'm with you,' he said.

'Enjoy your lunch,' I told him.

'And you eat yours up,' Beth told me. 'You're still much too thin. Are you warm enough?'

'I'm almost back to the weight I was when I joined the army,' I retorted, 'and I was just thinking of taking this coat off.' Even to myself I sounded petulant.

Charlie looked from one to the other of us with amuse-ment. Beth wiped the smile off his face. 'Isn't John too thin?' she demanded.

'Better that than too fat,' Charlie replied, tactfully and poetically.

'How true!' Isobel materialized out of the small throng which was centred on the buffet table. She had a loaded plate in one hand and a glass of what appeared to be gin in the other. 'I've just been ticking off one of the beaters because his dog's getting as fat as a pig despite all the work it gets. He'll have to harden his heart for the sake of the dog's if he doesn't want to lose it prematurely. And I was having a look at a tail.'

'Bad?' I asked.

'Horrid. There's a yellow Labrador in the line and each side of its chest was painted red. With blood,' she explained when Charlie looked blank. 'Instead of buggering about, stopping spaniels being docked, we should be recognizing that the day isn't far off when Labs should be docked as well.'

I could well understand the heat behind her words. Isobel had started life as a vet. Recently, Parliament had made it illegal for anyone except a qualified veterinary surgeon to dock a tail, despite the fact that breeders had for centuries been docking puppies within the first few days of life with so little ill effect that I had known the pup resume suckling within seconds.

The folly of that edict had been multiplied a thousand-fold when the Royal College of Veterinary Surgeons, rightly setting its face against docking for purely cosmetic reasons, had forbidden its members to do any docking at all except under conditions only likely to be encountered when the dog had reached a mature age, at which time docking would have become major surgery. And this had not been an idle tablet of stone but had been backed with threats of serious disciplinary action.

I was the principal trainer in the partnership, but Isobel, producing an unexpected talent and a cool head, had become the main handler under competition conditions, so she knew, perhaps better than any of us, that a gundog with an undocked tail worked in prickly cover (such as the gorse that abounds in our home territory and much of the rest of Britain) can strip the tip of its tail of hair, skin and even flesh. Beth's Labrador, Jason, was never worked on certain estates without a neat, leather sheath being taped onto his tail. So far from resenting or trying

12

to remove this appendage, he seemed to appreciate its purpose and stood like a statue for its attachment. This had at first been a matter for humour, but the sense of it had got through even to the mockers and we had had several enquiries from Labrador owners – so many, in fact, that Mrs Todd was now making them from soft rabbit-skin, for sale. But working spaniels are traditionally docked and Isobel had continued the practice on our pups. She was quite prepared, she said, to certify that each operation had been necessitated by injury and to dare the Royal College to do anything about it.

Jason was stretched out at Beth's feet, comfortably relaxing but ready to go again; but Clarence still stayed tight against Charlie's leg and I noticed that he shivered from time to time.

'Clarence isn't his usual boisterous self,' Isobel said to Charlie. 'Not infectious, is he?'

'Definitely not,' Charlie said with a lopsided smile. 'That I can guarantee.'

'That's good. I see,' she said, 'that you've had him docked. Who did it for you?'

'I've been wondering what was different about him,' I said. Looking more closely I saw that the white tip to what remained of Clarence's tail was white sticking plaster.

Charlie looked embarrassed. 'I'd rather not talk about it.'

'I shan't turn him in to the authorities,' Isobel said. When her professional interest is aroused she is not receptive to hints. 'I might ask him to join me in forming the Tail Dockers' Union. From what I can see, he's done a neat job, whoever he is. About a week ago?'

'About that,' Charlie agreed. 'I'm only letting Clarence off the lead in the open, well away from any kind of cover, until the stitches are out.'

'That's best,' Isobel said. 'Although whoever did the job took off rather more than I'd have cared to, which makes further damage unlikely. But I've hardly ever seen you send him into prickly cover. Was it some other kind of injury? I've known tails get slammed in car doors.'

Isobel's interest was in the general subject of docking rather than in Clarence but Charlie looked put out. 'I . . . As I said, I'd rather not talk about it,' he said gruffly.

We looked at each other in mild surprise. Dog-owners are usually as boring on the subject of their dogs' injuries as mothers about children's ailments. But Charlie was entitled to be reticent if he so wished. I made a guess that he had caused the injury by some piece of carelessness of which he was thoroughly ashamed and I changed the subject, conferring quickly with Isobel over the afternoon rota for the dogs.

Angus soon swept Isobel away to join the beating line again for the afternoon's drives, which would be down the other sides of the two valleys, and a few minutes later I marshalled the Guns and pickers-up.

The sun came out, brightening the scene. It also made life even more difficult for the Guns who were now facing it, but during the first two drives after lunch the shooting was almost good. As the looked-for total was neared, I placed the Guns closer to the foot of the slope where the birds would be highest and fastest. At the start of the eighth and final drive I placed myself, as promised, close behind Charlie Hopewell, making sure that he knew that I was there.

We still wanted seven birds. 'Take two,' I told Charlie. 'Then hold your fire.' He took his two. A dozen or more went over untouched but I saw three birds fall further along the line. The supply was running out. 'Two more,' I told Charlie. He scored a good right-and-left. They were almost the last birds to come over. Moments later the line of beaters punctuated the skyline. We ended the day with the exact hundred and fifty in the bag. Clarence, looking more confident than he had done all day, was allowed to help with the pick-up in the open.

I gathered the Guns together. 'You shot well, gentlemen,' I said. It was an exaggeration, but the clients appreciate an occasional compliment.

Back at the barn, Henry presided at the bar while I joined Angus, who was noting sexes and wing-tags for his records and setting aside braces of birds for the Guns – and for the beating team. (The beaters appreciated a brace of birds apiece, and in view of the low prices paid by the game-dealer our generosity cost us very little.)

Angus should have been happy at the end of a day which had been a triumph for him, but his moment had been spoiled. 'We've got at least one fox coming over the boundary again,' he said. 'The beaters found a little pile of wings and feathers. We've only lost a bird or two so far, but if it's a vixen and she sets up a den nearby we'll have a real problem in the spring.'

I could only agree. A vixen rearing cubs in the spring could wreak havoc among our nesting birds, and if she managed to dig her way into a release pen she could be counted on to slaughter every bird she could catch. I never blamed the fox, whose nature it was to grab an easy meal just as it was mine to defend my precious birds. The fox was part of nature's precarious balance, but so also were we. The neighbouring land was owned by an absentee landlord who would neither control foxes nor allow anybody else to do so on his land. An expensive battle might or might not have forced him to face up to his legal responsibilities. The only alternative lay in tactics of defence.

'What do you suggest?' I asked.

'I'll start a line of snares if you can take turns visiting them.'

I let out a sigh of relief. If Angus had asked for my help at lamping for the fox, as well he might, it would have meant nights of little or no sleep. But snares are at work while the keeper slumbers.

'We'll talk about it.' I picked out the largest and most magnificently coloured of the cocks. 'Include that in Mr Larrowby's brace. The man in the deerstalker hat. Tell him it's the one he shot on the first drive.'

'And is it?'

'Damned if I know. I lost track of his bird. But you'll make him happy and that'll be included in your tip.' Angus grinned and winked at me.

The yellow Labrador with the damaged tail had been withdrawn from the beating line early in the afternoon. Isobel was handing out free advice to its owner amid an interested group of Guns and beaters, most of whom had their own favourite remedies.

Charlie Hopewell, holding what looked like a large glass of whisky, stood slightly apart, Clarence staying close. I stopped beside them. 'That yellow bastard's lucky to have a tail to get skinned,' Charlie said thickly.

'No further damage to Clarence?' I asked.

Charlie shook his head. 'Maybe I should tell you what happened,' he said. 'But not here.' He led me away from the throng, pausing to have his now empty glass refilled on the way. We found seats in the barn. Clarence wedged himself between our legs. I could feel a tremor from his body. 'I didn't want to talk about it in front of strangers, but you've a right to know. I didn't have his tail docked. Some bastard just plain did it.'

'Did it?' I repeated stupidly.

'Chopped his tail off.' Charlie's voice, which had become shrill, returned to husky. 'You know what a wanderer he is?'

I said that I knew. A wanderer is usually incurable and by reputation Clarence was one of the worst. For days or weeks he would be faultless and then he would vanish. From heel, from home, out of his kennel or from the middle of a shoot, it made no difference.

'He's always been a wandering beggar,' Charlie said, not without a trace of quiet pride, 'and he makes enemies, no doubt about that. He's totally gut-oriented.'

'So are most dogs,' I pointed out.

'But with him it's an obsession. And he has the knack of making a quick raid on somebody's kitchen. He seems to believe that if he can get away he won't be identified. It's a belief that hasn't been shaken by the dozens of times an irate housewife has followed him home and I've had to punish him.'

'Clarence probably—'

Clarence made a small sound of distress and got to his feet. 'Try not to use his name,' Charlie said. 'He's still as friendly as ever and he can't help wagging his tail when he hears it, and if he does that while he's sitting down he hurts himself.'

I gave Clarence an apologetic pat. 'He probably thought that he was being punished for coming home.'

'I always take him back to where the crime was committed and punish him there. It never made any difference.'

'It probably wouldn't. Punishment has to follow close on the heels of the crime if it's to do any real good and not just relieve the victim's feelings.'

Charlie nodded and swallowed half his drink. 'It happened on the Friday, a week ago yesterday. He was in the house with me and he must have got out through a window. I didn't even know that he'd gone adrift until late morning when I heard him coming back, squealing. He was coming through the field, from this general direction as near as I could judge. There was blood all over and it took me a second or two to see what was wrong. Then I saw that a good half of his tail was missing and blood was dribbling from the severed end.'

Charlie gulped the last of his drink and pretended to blow his nose as a cover for wiping his eyes. 'God, it was awful! Hannah was weeping buckets, poor kid. She dotes on him, and I couldn't explain to her what I didn't understand myself.' He must have seen and misinterpreted some flicker of expression on my face because he flushed. 'I know term isn't finished yet,' he said. 'The fact is, she was ... sent home. She's past school-leaving age, so home's where I'm keeping her for the moment.

'Clarence didn't want to let me near the damage but I had to do something. I knew that I was hurting him although he behaved better than I probably would have done in the same circumstances. I got a tourniquet on it,

17

bundled him into the car. Hannah kept her head and held onto the tourniquet for me while I drove to the vet's surgery. They had to put him under and remove a little more in order to get enough skin to stitch over the bone. And of course they had to shave some of what was left. He still yelps if he bumps it against anything. And it looks terrible under the plaster.' Charlie looked as though he could weep at any moment.

'That's because you're used to seeing him with his tail complete. You hardly notice it, with the white sticking-plaster on it,' I said comfortingly, 'and it won't be notice-able at all when the hair grows in. Did you ever find out what had happened?'

'No. They said, at the vet's, that it had been something sharp and clean. That's all they could tell me.'

'He probably got caught up in some agricultural machinery.'

Charlie shook his head violently. 'There'd have been traces of rust or grease. Anyway, what machinery would have been working that day? It was pissing wet, re-member?'

When I thought about it, the season was long past when cutting machinery would have been in use in the fields. 'Do any of the local farmers have a machine to chop up turnips for the cattle?' I asked.

'Don't think so. Anyway, if he'd strayed into a barn and got his tail caught, I think they'd have told me. Damn it, I've been shooting pigeon and rabbit over their land for years with their full permission, not to say encouragement.'

I recognized the sensation in my lower stomach as apprehension. Or perhaps I was granted some foreknowl-edge of events to come. Whatever the reason, I did not at all like the way the conversation was heading. A working spaniel may be out of its owner's sight for minutes at a time. 'Who'd do such a thing?' I asked rhetorically.

Charlie shrugged. 'There are some bad buggers in the world,' he said. 'I'm wondering if it wasn't some anti-field-sports fanatic. Anyone who'll spray Antimate into the eyes of a hound wouldn't stop there.' He sighed deeply.

He was putting my worst fears into words. 'You need another drink,' I said. I fetched one from Henry's stock and collected a small one for myself. I had been teetotal for long enough and Beth could probably be persuaded to drive.

Charlie accepted the drink gratefully. 'When I was a young man,' he said, 'I thought of myself as an intellectual. I listened to music and looked at paintings and sculpture and I read all the great works. I studied architecture and I made a living and stuck it for a thirty-year career. It soon stopped meaning very much to me but at least it furnished the wherewithal for an early retirement.

'And that's when I realized what I should have known all along – that I'm a creature of primitive instincts, like most of the human race. What I really enjoy, as opposed to what gives me mild amusement, is pursuit of my meat. After all, to our remote ancestors – animal and human – the hunt and the subsequent celebration in the form of a feast were the high points of life. So I shoot, I fish, I work in harmony with my dog, and if I can't do the same in heaven I don't want to go there. Am I so wicked?' He looked at me owlishly. He was becoming slightly drunk.

'Not in my book,' I said, rather dazed by this sudden outpouring from a usually reticent man. I was also feeling my apprehension growing. If an anti-field-sports fanatic was becoming active against gundogs in the area, our kennels would be high on the target list. And the fanatics, who were given to such activities as desecrating graves and releasing mink into the countryside, had, as Charlie said, not shown any qualms about attacking dogs. Whenever a dog was maimed, until the culprit was caught, I always lived in hourly expectation of disaster.

'I don't know what they're on about,' Charlie resumed gloomily. 'It's not as if many of them are vegetarian. They don't mind sinking their teeth into a bird which has been reared in semi-darkness, never been out of a cage in its life and has been slaughtered, with minimal consideration, as soon as it's old enough to eat. Yet they bitterly resent my shooting a bird which was released into the wild for that very purpose and has had at least a few months, possibly several seasons, to enjoy it, and which stands at least an even chance of living to enjoy one or two more.'

I looked round, but the socializing was still going on around the mobile bar and Angus was filling out game-cards. 'Do you remember an old song of the Beverly Sisters?' I asked Charlie. 'The recurring theme was, "If there's something you enjoy you can be certain that . . . It's illegal, it's immoral or it makes you fat." If to illegality, immorality or high calories you add undesirability, I go along with it all the way.'

'You surely don't include field sports as undesirable?' Charlie asked.

'No, of course not. I was thinking that, for anyone who doesn't do anything himself, the most fun that he gets is interfering with the activities of anyone he doesn't agree with, whether or not he understands them. That's what I was calling undesirable.'

'But why do they enjoy it?' Charlie asked again. 'Why?'

It was a subject to which I had given some thought. Charlie, who was working the depression out of his system, deserved an answer. 'Nearly a hundred years ago,' I said, 'things changed. But up until then the nobs, who were also the rich, could spend most of their lives hunting or shooting, and so of course they tried to keep it for themselves. Naturally. That's how things were in those days. Poaching was savagely put down.

'That all altered early this century, with changes both in the law and social reform. But attitudes don't change as quickly. They get handed down from generation to generation, not necessarily in words – a frown or a sniff is enough to tell a child what its parents think. So, to the left-wing city-dweller, shooting is still the rich man's privilege and never mind that you and I have shot with chefs and window-cleaners. What gives credibility to that view is that good, driven shooting, like today's, does cost money.' I punched my own knee, quite painfully. 'Of course it bloody does! If you want the best of anything, be it a car or a watch, a wine or a woman, you pay accordingly. But if you happen to have the money and you choose to spend it on a Rolex or a Ferrari, the bigots don't give a tuppenny fart. But just try spending it on conservation on a grouse moor . . .'

'Cool down,' Charlie said, half laughing. 'I'm the one with the excuse to get hot under the collar. I only told you so's you'd be careful.'

I took several deep breaths and began, as he said, to cool down. 'We'll be careful,' I promised. 'But it was a damnable thing to happen.' Another thought came unbidden into my mind. 'A nutter running around attacking spaniels would provide a perfect alibi for owners who want to get around the new legislation.' Charlie suddenly became very white and looked as though he might be sick at any moment. He turned his back quickly on where the rest of the company were laughing and chatting. 'Don't take me seriously,' I said. 'I was only making a stupid joke to lighten the atmosphere.'

'You weren't to know,' he said. He looked up into the rafters of the barn and went on very quickly in a choked voice. 'But the whole business has brought me nothing but trouble. Quite apart from the pain to Buggins here – ' he pointed down at Clarence ' – and the shock to us all. He injured his tail once before and I consulted my vet – McMahon – about docking. But McMahon's is mostly a farm animal practice and he turned out to be fanatically opposed to docking. He lectured me for an hour on it being a prime instance of the sacrifice of a dog on the altar of the vanity of dog-owners. Then I had to take the dog to him to . . . to tidy up the mess and I think he must have tipped off the police and the SSPCA, because they've been harassing the hell out of me and I know they've been asking around about my views on the question of docking. They must think I chopped my own dog's tail off so that

21

McMahon would have to make a proper job of docking it.'

'Nobody who knows you would believe such a thing,' I said.

'But what about those who don't know me? A sheriff, for example?' he asked.

'They surely can't drum up enough evidence for a prosecution.'

'Not yet,' Charlie said glumly. 'But they're getting bits and pieces. The lady next door, for instance. We'd fallen out over trivial things – I had to speak to her about popping slugs over the fence. What made it more annoying is that I rather like her, quite apart from the fact that she's the best-looking woman for miles around.' Charlie still looked moody but a hand came up, without intention on his part, to give his moustache a twirl. 'She's been telling them that she heard him squeal. Well, of course, he did squeal while I was applying the tourniquet but, the way she tells it, you could believe that he was screaming in agony.'

I wanted to break off the discussion which was making me feel slightly sick, but I had an idea that talking about it into a sympathetic ear was doing Charlie some good. 'Couldn't you show them the trail of blood arriving?' I asked. 'Or even track it back to where it happened?'

'I tried. But the rain had washed any traces away. And then I tried taking him for walks, to see if any particular place gave him the collywobbles.'

'And did it?'

'He's still scared to go most places outside the house. When I want to walk him, I have to take him out in the car first. He seems to like it here. He associates this place with happy times, so he's a lot more confident and relaxed.'

Here at least I could help. 'Walk him here any time,' I said. 'I'll tell Angus.'

'Thanks.'

'Has it stopped him wandering?'

'For the moment. It won't last,' Charlie said gloomily.

I could think of nothing useful to say. The company was preparing to break up. 'Come and collect your brace of birds,' I said. 'And then I think we'd better run you home. Unless you're joining the others at the hotel?'

'Drop us at home,' he said. 'I'm not in the mood for dining out and Hannah will be looking for me.' He shook hands politely all round, tipped Angus and put Clarence into the back of my car.

I let the pair of them out at Charlie's front gate. Hannah must have been watching from a neighbour's house, because she was on the scene before Clarence, who was being careful not to knock his tail, had made a cautious descent from the car. A pretty girl with all the physical charm that belongs to girls in their late teens, her manner towards her father was reserved but I had never seen much sign of the rebelliousness which worried Charlie so much. My own reading would have been that she was ready to throw off the shackles of family and school and had not yet learned restraint. She seemed to be happy by nature and had an infectious smile when she cared to use it. I thought that if Charlie would treat her as a full-blown adult she could respond. It might not yet be too late.

'You could take her to the dinner,' I said. 'The others wouldn't mind.'

Charlie shook his head without speaking. I thought that he was perhaps being too sensitive. But Hannah was his daughter, not mine, and there were so many traps into which a parent could fall. I felt a sudden clutch of fear for Sam.

Hannah knelt down beside Clarence and wrapped her arms around him. Clarence tried to restrain his tail but it wagged in spite of him.

Hannah looked up at her father. 'He's all right?' she asked sternly.

'He's fine, Poppet.' Charlie gathered up his gun and his brace of birds. 'Take him inside and we'll give him his dinner.'

The three of them went into their house without looking back.

23

TWO

Angus was waiting impatiently for his wife in his Land
Rover outside our house. The invaluable Mrs Todd had
taken several messages, fed the puppies and kept Sam's
body and his soul together, but there were a host of tasks
which we could neither ask nor expect her to undertake.
Beth dashed around in a whirl of activity, dealing with
Sam and the dogs and somehow contriving to whizz a
meal through the microwave, assisted by Isobel and, after
the nap which they combined to force on me, myself. We
ate, rather after our usual time but happy in the recollection of a successful day during which none of the dogs
had erred more than we could rectify within the week;
and our clients had been pleased.

Our one customary indulgence at Three Oaks was for
the partners, plus Henry and anybody else who happened
to be around, to settle in the sitting room when the work
was done, to mull over the day gone by and to plan for
the future over a drink which was, by then, overdue after
a day of sustained and often sober effort. Henry, who had
an uncanny instinct in such matters, had been hosting
the visitors at dinner but arrived by taxi as I poured
the drinks.

At first we were content to enjoy the deep chairs and
the firelight and to congratulate ourselves that another
perilous day had gone by without a serious hitch. Nobody
had behaved dangerously, no dogs had run riot (except
that Phinny had taken off after a rabbit which bolted
from under her nose and she had ignored the stop whistle

24

for the first few yards of the chase. It had been a small fault but one which would ruin her chances in competition. Some one-on-one retraining in the rabbit pen would be necessary, followed by a careful reintroduction to the real world). We moved on to plan ahead.

The last few weeks of the season were almost on us. There would be a short break in the competition programme over the festive season – to allow the judges to recover from the effects of all the gifted bottles, so it was said – after which would come the biggest stakes of the year, climaxing for us in the Spaniel Championship. Meanwhile, at Foleyknowe, the most important shoots of the year were still to come and would have to be managed with equal precision and good fortune if the shoot's accounts were to finish in the black for the year. Had we bitten off too much, we wondered sleepily? Time would tell.

Time would also produce fresh problems. Our legislators, together with the Ministry, had made obligatory the European concept of setaside land. This they (the legislators and the Ministry) were hailing as a masterly step towards wildlife conservation; but in a single stroke they had snatched disaster from the jaws of success by decreeing that setaside land, after being left wild to attract all the wildlife in the area, should be mown to the ground just when it would be full of nesting birds and hares with young – and again in July, in case any had escaped.

Over the second or third round of drinks, discussion of this piece of bureaucratic brilliance and of various ways by which we might at least try to minimize the damage to our wild stock of pheasants naturally led Isobel to her hobby-horse of tail-docking. I had meant to keep the story of Clarence to myself, but once Isobel had revealed as much as she knew about it, it was impossible for me not to tell the rest.

Beth was a fervent advocate of the docking of working spaniels, but she was always the first by a short head to empathize with an injured dog. She exploded. Only a

25

bloody-minded, sadistic psychopath, she said hotly, would even contemplate committing such an outrage.

I was inclined to agree. I had a feeling that we were seeing the tip of a very nasty iceberg, although at the time I had no way of knowing how nasty. The others couldn't quite go so far. Henry expressed it for us. 'You may be right,' he told Beth. 'On the other hand, if there is such a psychopath around it's remarkable that he has only broken out to the extent of one spaniel's tail. After all, there are other possible explanations. Not probable ones, I hasten to add, but no less unlikely than your sadistic, bloody-minded psychopath.'

Beth snorted in disgust. 'I defy you to think of anything even faintly conceivable,' she said angrily, waving her hands and spilling sherry.

Isobel had been watching with amusement as the argument developed. 'Hold your horses,' she said. 'Don't I remember something about Charlie having a rather wild daughter?'

Beth's face dropped. 'I'd forgotten,' she said. 'How awful! I met her once. She seemed such a nice girl.'

The idea of Hannah as the assailant had no sooner entered Beth's head than it had begun to take root. I realized suddenly that Charlie's defensive attitude towards Hannah had been out of fear that the same reaction would be general. 'I've met her several times,' I said. 'She's never misbehaved while I was there, but piecing together what Charlie told me and what I've heard around, she's going through the rebellious phase that we all went through at some point in our teens. She's slightly hyperactive and definitely over-emotional and I've heard stories of a temper which she's only just learning to control. But she's not daft. Not as daft as Clarence, to be honest.'

'All the same,' Beth said, 'although I hate to say it, and I can't imagine that sweet girl taking a knife to Clarence, it does make a sort of sense. Dogs can be damned annoying if you don't understand how their minds work. Clarence annoyed her and the famous temper went off pop.'

'I'll bet you the neighbours are saying the same thing. I think that that's what's worrying Charlie most. Not that he thinks that she could have done it – she loves Clarence and he seemed pleased to see her – but that it may spoil her relationships with other people and set back her development.'

'I see all that,' said Beth. 'I wouldn't have believed her capable of such a thing. Yet I don't believe that there's any more credible explanation.'

'Do you want to make a bet on it?' Henry asked.

'Definitely no,' I said quickly. Beth would have felt obliged to back her honour, but I had no wish to see our precious funds diverted in the direction of Henry, who never made a bet unless he was very confident of winning it.

'A pity,' Henry said. 'Never mind. Let's look at it methodically, all the same. One, somebody had a grudge against Clarence or wanted to deter him from paying any more visits. Is Clarence a randy dog?'

'Charlie told me that he was,' said Beth. 'He seemed quite proud of him. Owners usually are. And it's usually true, because most male dog's are randy by nature.'

'I can confirm it, in Clarence's case,' I said. 'I've seen him try to mate with a dead vixen.'

'There you are, then. Some owner of a bitch or bitches got fed up with Clarence coming around with an evil gleam in his eye. Cutting off his tail was a rather ruthless way of saying, "And don't come back", and rather less drastic than murder or castration. That's more believable than a psychopath, isn't it?'

'Much,' I said.

'And more credible than the Hopewell girl being the culprit?'

'That also.'

Although he was stretched out in his chair so that his long legs almost crossed the room, Henry managed to sketch a bow. 'Two,' he said, 'somebody has a grudge against Clarence's owner. I remember him. A mild man, but even mild men can make enemies. It could have been a threatening gesture or a secretive way of hurting him, but it might even turn out to be a subtle way of trying to provoke him. I have known such a thing. If somebody had a motive, such as an impending legal action, for wanting friend Charlie to blot his copy-book . . .'

'I think my psychopath's more likely than that,' Beth growled.

'Perhaps it's my devious mind at work,' Henry conceded cheerfully. 'We'll let that one stick to the wall. Three, conceive of somebody on the run, perhaps an escaped prisoner. He's hiding out in a barn or shed when Clarence comes round and won't go away.

'Then, four, let's consider accidents.'

'Oh, come on,' Beth said. 'You can't cut off a dog's tail accidentally.'

'It's possible,' I said. 'But, Henry, it was a soaking wet day. Nobody would have taken out a tractor or tried to cut silage, anything like that – even if it was the right time of year, which it wasn't.'

'If a man's hand or foot can be cut off accidentally,' Henry said, 'so can a dog's tail. Imagine a chainsaw. Or a man using one of those petrol-driven brush-cutters, like a strimmer with a saw blade instead of the nylon cord. They're noisy, so the operator has no warning. Imagine it. Say the dog's hiding under a bush with just his tail sticking out. Or the dog comes running, tries to turn away but skids down a muddy bank. The man's left with a severed tail. He doesn't want any trouble and he doesn't know whose dog it was anyway. The dog can't give evidence against him. He tosses the tail into the boiler or buries it and says nothing.'

'You may as well stop droning on now,' Isobel said. 'I think you've made your point.'

Henry grinned at her. He had a startlingly youthful grin for such a well-worn face. 'I've almost finished. I'll offer you one more suggestion. The vet said that it was a clean cut. But you open up a much wider field of possibilities if you think of somebody trying to cover up some other accident. Imagine, for instance, somebody engaged in an illegal activity. Poaching, perhaps. Clarence's tail gets punctured by a two-two bullet or caught in an illegal trap. Or – ' Henry's face lit up ' – soaked in blood. Would he come to a stranger?'

I thought back to my few previous encounters with Clarence. 'I think so,' I said. 'He's soft and trusting. If he'd been hurt or frightened he might go to the nearest human being for comfort and reassurance, especially if that person called to him in the right tone of voice.'

'But there's been no murder or assault around here,' Isobel said.

I felt a momentary shiver run up my back.

'Not that we know of as yet,' Henry said with relish. 'Perhaps somebody has good reason not to want the occurrence revealed. And what better way would there be of covering up blood splashes on a dog? Our hypothetical assailant could hardly give Clarence a forcible bath. If it makes you feel better, Beth, consider that it would be better than killing the dog and burying him quietly in the corner of a field.'

'Well, I still think that only a psychopath could do a thing like that,' Beth said defiantly.

'And Charlie's daughter isn't one of those,' I said. 'She may be wild but there's never been any suggestion that she was evil.'

'Psychopaths are very clever about not showing it,' Beth said.

'Whoever did it, psychopath or not,' I said, 'I'll be happier in my mind when we know who and why.'

'Time we were going,' Henry said without moving. 'We've thought before now that somebody might be developing a spite against working spaniels. It always turned out to be a one-off.'

'There was that old lady who was trying to make a bob or two breeding Pekes,' Beth said sleepily. 'She went berserk when Samson put her prize bitch in the family way.'

'The worst that she ever did was to swipe at spaniels with her handbag,' Isobel reminded her. 'The truth will probably emerge of its own accord. But if it'll set our minds at rest, John may as well ask a few questions. Come on, Henry. We're walking home.'

We gave ourselves our usual easy Sunday, or as easy as a day can be with so many runs to be kept clean and so many hungry mouths ready to object loudly if their normal feeding time should be delayed by even a minute. The rest of the day was nominally free time, which meant that Beth spent it gardening with Sam nearby while I was eradicating any faults which had shown up among dogs in training, especially the impetuous Phinny (short for Delphinium). Isobel came over and updated her comprehensive records of gundog bloodlines.

On Monday, it was back to work with a vengeance. Angus Todd phoned. 'You want to meet me over at Foleyknowe?' It was a statement rather than a question. 'I'm putting out a line of snares. If you gi'e me a hand you'll ken where they are.'

I could well have done without the distraction, but Angus was perfectly right to remind me that we were obliged to free him to pursue his other careers as goose guide and small-scale game-farmer when required. If a fox was making inroads into our pheasants, a line of snares was only sensible, but the law required that they be visited at least once a day; and a party of Guns planning a winter's break had booked Angus's services in pursuit of the Tay geese from the Tuesday to the Friday prior to Foleyknowe's driven pheasants on the Saturday. They would have been happy enough to come to Foleyknowe a day earlier, which would have suited us very well, but we knew that, while we could easily obtain promises, assembling a team of reliable beaters during the week was almost impossible.

I looked at the clock. 'Would eleven-thirty be time enough?' I asked Angus.

'Just about. If I've already set off, I'll have left the ATV for you and I'll be on the northern march.'

'I'll catch up with you,' I told him.

We broke the connection and I went to tell Beth that I would be out to lunch.

Beth had only one concern, far above foxes, dog-training or help with the chores. 'You will eat properly?' she asked anxiously.

'I'll have a pub lunch,' I said. 'I'll take a couple of dogs with me and stay on to give some extra training. I'll be back around dusk.'

Two dogs would be as much as I could manage if I had to ride Angus's ATV, which was one of those go-anywhere four-wheel motorbikes so popular with keepers and farmers. Phinny would need another session in the rabbit pen before she could be trusted again on the loose; even one more misdeed might serve to ingrain the bad habit. We settled that I would take Fern, a young bitch getting a final polish for a client, and Conker, a slightly older dog destined to graduate to stud if he made a good enough showing at the forthcoming Spaniel Championship, for which he had already qualified. He was a brilliant performer but given to occasional lapses. It was a pity, I thought, that there was no way of making him understand the delights in store for him if he would only concentrate and remember all that he had been taught . . .

Beth went through the usual rigmarole of checking that I was warmly wrapped and that I had money, my pills and towels for the dogs. Her solicitude used to annoy me but I had come to recognize it as stemming from anxiety mixed with love and to realize that I would be desperately hurt if it should ever cease. I bore it patiently, got away almost on time and arrived at Foleyknowe on the dot of eleven-thirty.

Between the big house and the stubble where we had parked the cars was a woodland strip of mature, mixed

conifers. We had the use of a brick shed almost hidden by rhododendrons among the trees, and here Angus stored feed for the pheasants, along with any traps, pen sections, feeders and tools not in immediate use. Angus was loading bags of grain into his Land Rover. The ATV was still in the shed. I parked nearby. 'With a bit of luck we can take this beast all the way,' Angus said, patting his elderly Land Rover affectionately. 'Chuck your dogs in the back. There's still room.'

I accepted lifts to the top of the first hill for myself and the two dogs and brought my bagged gun out of the car. Even in four-wheel drive the Land Rover slithered on the muddy tracks and damp grass. The cattle had been taken under cover by now but there were sheep in the fields and I had to climb in and out on gate duty. The still-unploughed stubbles were easier going, but Angus was sweating under his waxproofed coat by the time he had wrestled the heavy vehicle onto the crest. It occurred to me that he might have put out less effort to walk up, grain and all. I watched him set six snares along an obvious fox route where there were signs of recent droppings.

The drinking points had refilled automatically during the recent rain with water from the roofs of the low shelters. Angus topped up the feeding hoppers with grain while I hunted the dogs among the gorse. The pheasants were still too precious an asset to be squandered in train-ing, although the cocks would become expendable in a month or so; but there were rabbits in plenty and it was easy to miss the birds with a shot or two but give a few retrieves on the bunnies. It was all valuable steadiness training and the two dogs came out of it well, hunting close, dropping to flush or to shot and retrieving to hand in fine style. Without counting any chickens I had hopes of a successful January to start another year.

A keen wind was slicing across the hilltop. Back in the Land Rover, Angus produced a flask of hot coffee and we sat for a minute warming our hands on the mugs, looking down over our territory and comparing notes. A

different pattern of drives would be needed if the ground was to be driven again only a week after the previous shoot, but before the coffee was gone we had made our tentative plans, subject to the weather on the day.

While we crossed a saddle to the next crest, Angus could relax and listen for a moment, so I told him about Clarence's misadventure. Angus had been my sergeant in the Falklands and I knew him for a tough and unsentimental character, but even so he managed to surprise me.

'Maybe that'll learn the bugger,' he said.

'Teach him what?' I said, trying not to sound as though I was correcting Angus's syntax.

'To stay at home instead of stravaiging all over the countryside. A confirmed wanderer is that dog. Many's the time I've seen him in our cover here after the rabbits, though he never caught one to my knowledge. I've never seen him chase a pheasant either,' Angus admitted handsomely, 'although that's not to say he never does it.' He glanced sideways and saw me looking at him. 'I didn't trim his tail for him – never got close enough – so don't put it down to me.'

'Who do you think I should put it down to?'

Angus had to give his full attention to wrestling the Land Rover through a gate in a dip and round the end of an old stone wall. A small flock of pheasants were sunning themselves in the middle of the track, sheltered by a broom-covered mound; they were less tame than they would have been a month or two earlier but even so they scurried out of the way at their own pace and Angus had to slow down just where he would have liked to keep going. As one, the birds suddenly took off. I thought that they must have heard what Angus was calling them under his breath. All four wheels span before he could nurse us up and round.

Then we were at the next feeding area. I gave the dogs another workout while Angus filled the feeders and a large storage bin and checked on the water supply. Any old fox-tracks were indistinct. Angus produced a brush-cutter from the back of his Land Rover, fired up the two-stroke motor and cut back the cover by which a fox could have crept up on the feeding birds. When I rejoined him he was setting snares in a pathway which he had cut for the purpose.

'I suppose Clarence didn't back into your brush-cutter?' I suggested.

Angus looked at me, wondering whether to take offence and indulge in one of his occasional, calculated flare-ups. But he knew that I can give as good as I get in that department; and years of habit, NCO to officer, may have tipped the balance.

'I don't have accidents,' he said, quite mildly for him. 'I'm too bloody careful. And any bits I chop off that bugger on purpose will be off the other end.' He looked at me again, more searchingly. 'Here, you're getting cold. Your lady'll take the brush-cutter and chop lumps off *me* if I let you freeze. Get back in the Land Rover. I've finished here and that's as many snares as you'll want to visit in a day. The birds'll be disturbing them and half of them'll have to be reset.' He spoke gruffly and I thought that his concern was genuine and that he would set twice as many snares as soon as he was doing the visiting himself.

I was glad to get in out of the cold. Angus dropped his brush-cutter beside the dogs in the now almost empty back of the mud-plastered Land Rover and joined me.

'You never answered my question,' I said as we rolled down another track.

'What question was that?'

'I asked you who you thought I should put Clarence's docking down to.'

Angus shrugged and then caught the resulting swerve. 'I don't know many of the beggars around here. Just the two farmers, and either one of them could have got sick of wandering dogs coming around. I'm not saying that Clarence would have worried sheep, spaniels aren't bad that way, but dogs are pack animals and there'd always

34

be the risk that he'd bring a companion with him, a terrier maybe or a collie. That was my fear with the pheasants. Then there's the owners of any bitches in season. He's a devil for wandering, that Clarence – looking to get his leg over, most often. And he'd steal food quick as look at it. 'A good worker when his mind's on the job, I'll say that for him,' Angus added fairly. As keeper, Angus had mostly seen Clarence in the beating line where little more would be asked of him than to crash through the bushes to push the birds out. 'And I've time for Mr Hopewell, he's a gent, but there it is. I've no difficulty picturing in my mind almost anybody taking a hasty scliff at Clarence with a knife, say, or a pruning hook, not meaning any great harm but lashing out in irritation and forgetting for the moment what it is that he has in his hand. You see what I mean?'

I said that I could see exactly what Angus meant. 'You don't suppose that Charlie could have made up the story to explain an illicit tail-docking when the SSPCA came after him?'

'Doubt it,' Angus said. 'If he kept him undocked to – what? – about four years old, why for would he suddenly dock him now? He doesn't do enough hunting to skin his tail in the gorse, the way yours would. If you're looking that near to home – which I'm no' suggesting you should – it's no' Mr Hopewell you should be looking at.'

I did not want to hear any more. Changing a subject with Angus was like trying to divert a runaway train, but I managed it somehow.

We had covered the salient parts of the northern boundary – which adjoined the forestry and the source of any wandering foxes – from east to west and we were descending close to the other branch of the local road, which formed our eastern boundary. From the village, it was signposted to Kirkton of Littleknapp, wherever that might be, but it seemed to be heading in a general direction between Perth and Coupar Angus.

A broad dam screened by trees winked in sudden sunshine. At a cost of little more than a few days of a bull-dozer, we had dammed the burn and flooded some waste ground. The duck, both released and wild, formed a useful addition to a shooting day.

'Do you want to give the dogs some water-work?' Angus asked. 'I could let you out here.'

'Not today,' I said. 'These two are good in water and I don't want them wet for the rest of the day.'

'A pity.' We turned into the track along the bottom of the valley, scattering ahead of us more pheasants which had come out to enjoy the sun. 'Those duck get too damn tame. If you get the chance later in the week, have the dogs chase them around a bit.'

'I'll remember. Are you coming for lunch at the pub?'

'Better not,' he said reluctantly. 'I've the rest of the feeders to fill, and then I'd best be off home and get everything ready. Somehow getting up and about before dawn isn't quite the fun it used to be. When we were in the Regiment, I swore that once I was out I'd never get up early again, and here I am doing it off my own bat with-out even a bugler to wake me.' He yawned at the thought.

'You know you love it,' I said to encourage him. The present arrangement was too well-balanced for me to risk allowing him to throw it up in a fit of despondency. The combination of a day at the driven pheasants with several days wildfowling or rough-shooting was proving to be a popular winter break for busy, middle-income men and provided an invaluable shop-window for the dogs. 'Have you found anything for your visitors to do on the spare day?' I asked.

'I offered them another day on the foreshore, but they wanted to take it easy before the pheasants,' he said disgustedly. It was all right, apparently, for Angus to feel his age; sedentary office workers, it seemed, should be made of sterner stuff. 'If I can spot any kale being vandal-ized, I'll see if I can't settle them down for a day in pigeon hides, shooting over decoys. Then I'll go back to my bed.'

'Will you be going anywhere off-road during the week?' I asked him.

'Nowhere your car couldn't manage. You want the Land Rover? Daft question,' he said quickly, laughing at himself. 'Of course you do. I'll meet you back here and we'll swap. Two-thirtyish?'

'Fine,' I said.

He pulled up beside my car. I transferred my gun and the dogs into it and a few minutes later I parked on the tarmac forecourt of the local hotel. The hotel was small, having grown from being a modest village pub by dint of several extensions, but it was one of the new generation of smaller Scottish hotels, aspiring to a standard of comfort, décor and cuisine that a few years earlier would have been exclusive to the largest of city hotels. The original building had been gloomy and now was only relieved by pale paint and bright lights; but the main bar was in an extension with wide windows and a view to the Sidlaw Hills. The hotel garden, spread outside the windows, had been intelligently landscaped and even now, outside the flowering season, it was cheerful with variegated foliage and the bright stems of dogwood.

On previous visits I had made do with the soup and crusty bread; but fresh air and exercise had roused my sluggish appetite and I ordered Guinness and the scampi. The latter arrived in quantity, complete with generous portions of chips and salad. Slightly daunted, I set to work on it, and had reduced the mountain to a mere hillock of chips when a stocky male figure loomed over me.

I looked up. Charlie Hopewell was regarding me from behind his generous nose. He was dressed comfortably but was much too smart for a shooting day, which was how I had always seen him in recent years. 'Join you for a moment?' he asked.

'Of course. For lunch?'

He dropped into a chair. 'I've eaten.'

'But you don't have a drink,' I said. I turned to try and catch the eye of a waitress.

'Nothing for me,' Charlie said hastily. 'There'll be plenty where I'm going. I tried to phone you at home but they said that you'd either be on the shoot or lunching here. John, I'm in a pickle.'

I pushed my plate away. 'Tell me about it.'

Charlie looked distressed. 'Don't let me spoil your lunch.'

'I've already eaten twice my usual,' I assured him. 'I feel pregnant.' I began work on the remains of my Guinness.

'I hope it's a pretty one. That's all right, then. Listen, will you keep Clarence for me for a few days?'

The last thing that we would want about the place would be a traumatized, non-breeding resident, not bringing in training fees and subject to aberrations of wandering and lust. 'We don't usually take boarders,' I said carefully.

Charlie looked horrified. 'Please,' he said. 'I've got to leave within the hour if I'm to catch my plane. Hannah can go to my neighbour – not the sexy one, the one the other side – but I don't know what to do about Clarence. The nearest kennels had him once before and he came back with fleas and kennel cough. There's another place he's been at, but they said they wouldn't have him again at any price. He got out of his run, last time, pinched the family's Sunday dinner and – oh – raped the cat or something, I don't know what, they wouldn't even talk about it.'

'Can't he stay where he is? Hannah could feed him and walk him.'

'I couldn't count on it. Mrs Turner – the neighbour – means well, but she'd insist on taking over and she'd let him loose. I can't dent her conviction that Clarence will do whatever she tells him.'

'You're not making a very good case for him,' I said.

'I'm being honest. And showing need. Besides, you can cope, you're famous for it. The other neighbour, the gorgeous one, used to look after him for short periods if my son was away, but I can't ask her now.' Charlie blew a sigh which was almost a raspberry. 'I don't know who she thinks she is, her husband's only a postman.'

38

'An expensive area for a postman, isn't it?' I asked.

'There was some money came with her, from what I heard. Probably her dad paid him to take her away – she has trouble written all over her, or as much of her as I've been able to study so far. Listen, I don't have time to shop around, and anyway I don't want Clarence too near here while he's frightened, and for all I know somebody may be after him. I know you'd keep him safe and try to calm him down. You'll do it?'

'Hold your horses,' I said. 'What's the sudden panic? We have a rule about not taking in boarders, and if I break it I'll never be able to control Beth next time she takes pity on some widow with an overweight poodle and an invitation to Brighton for a dirty weekend.' This last had been an actual example.

Charlie cast an anguished glance at his watch. 'The panic,' he said, 'is that my son and his wife, who usually take Clarence for me if I'm going away, went for a winter break in the French Alps and they got more break than they bargained for. My son broke his leg skiing and his wife doesn't drive. He's got unmissable business appointments next week and they've made a balls of the travel insurance, so I've got to fly out and chauffeur the pair of them home.'

I hardened my heart. 'Tell him to fly home and he can go back for his car after he's got his cast off,' I suggested.

'But he took my car,' Charlie said simply.

'That's different.' I gave the matter some serious thought. I would have to help him out but at least I could extract a substantial quid pro quo. 'I'll tell you what I'll do,' I said at last. 'I'll look after Clarence at no charge if you'll do me a favour in return.'

'Anything. Within reason,' Charlie added hastily.

'It's within reason all right,' I told him. 'We've got a real log-jam coming up in January. We've got a dog qualified to run in the Spaniel Championship. That takes Isobel and Beth away. We've also entered two of the cockers in a puppy stake, which we'd hoped would set at least one of

39

them on the track for next year, and that happens to coincide with the second day of the Championship. I was going to do that one, but it looked as though we were going to have to cancel, because a corporate booking came in for the shoot for the same day. One of the oil companies entertaining visiting American consultants. All the money in the world and just when we had a flat spot in the bookings. We simply can't afford to let it escape.'

'And where would I come in?' Charlie asked suspiciously.

'You run the shoot that day.'

The look of horror on his face would have been excessive if I had suggested that he drive in a Grand Prix or run for Queen. 'I couldn't manage it,' he said earnestly. 'I wouldn't know how.'

'Nothing to it,' I said. 'Angus will control the beating line. All you do is meet the visitors, make sure that lunch is booked, collect the balance of the money, let them draw numbers, place the Guns however Angus has told you, dish out cartridges and make sure they get three hundred birds, not less and not too many more. They're all experienced shots so you won't have to worry about novices. You can shoot with them if you want,' I added as an irresistible inducement. 'And at the end, tell them how brilliantly they did, hand out a brace of birds apiece and take a brace for yourself.'

'Is that all?' Charlie asked weakly.

'Almost. Act as barman between drives, but you may have Henry to help you there. We'll arrange for several pickers-up, you just have to time things so that the pickers-up can hunt for any pricked birds and catch up again in time for the next drive. Pay off the beaters and the pickers-up and give them a brace each. Hand over the rest of the birds to the game-dealer. Solve any problems and deal with any complaints. If anybody gets dangerously fu', send him to sit in one of the cars. I'll write it all out for you.'

Charlie was looking horrified again. 'I couldn't order a rich American to go and sit in a car!'

'If he's had too much to drink and he's waving a shot-gun around, all the others will back you up. Even Americans take loaded guns seriously. Will you do it or won't you?'

'Oh God! I suppose so.' Charlie was looking past me. 'Here's my taxi. Clarence is in his kennel behind my house. You can collect him.'

'Wait,' I said. I slapped a pen and a used envelope down on the table. 'Write me out some sort of a note, in case somebody asks me why I'm stealing a spaniel.' Charlie dithered between complying and rushing for his taxi. 'Otherwise,' I said, 'I'll just tell them that you're paying me to take him away and abandon him on the M90. They'd believe that.'

Charlie uttered a rude word and grabbed up the pen.

'Tell me one thing,' I said. I hardened my heart. 'Where was Hannah when Clarence's tail was cut off?'

Charlie jumped so that a perfect symbol for a hiccup appeared on the paper. He glared at me, but decided that to protest might be to rock the boat. 'She was with me,' he said stoutly. I did not believe him, but I thought that he had chosen the answer for its brevity rather than for any other reason.

The heart of the village, clustered around a small green in front of the hotel, was built of small stone houses and a pair of shops, with tall trees and the spire of a church for background. More modern if less picturesque houses had been added on the outskirts and Charlie's house, as I remembered from the previous Saturday, was in a cul-de-sac of detached bungalows behind the hotel. His back windows looked across a patchwork of fields to the rising ground where our shoot began.

I parked in the short drive, took out one of the nylon slip-leads with which my car is always well-provided and walked round the house.

The accommodation that Charlie had supplied for Clarence stood in the corner of a back garden that was mostly grass with a surrounding border. It had begun as a wooden

kennel in a conventional run of chicken wire. The wire
had later been reinforced with welded mesh and the
whole run had been added to or reinforced, using a
variety of materials, whenever Clarence had made his
escape over, under or through the wire, until now it would
surely have been proof against anything from a swarm of
bees to a grizzly bear. Only a Chubb lock was lacking,
but I had to draw back no fewer than four big bolts
before I could drag open the gate of heavy piping and
corrugated metal.

Clarence had retired deep inside the kennel. I could
have opened the back of the kennel but, remembering
the attack that he had recently suffered, I judged that he
would be less frightened if I stooped to the small doorway
and made coaxing noises, hoping that he would soon
recognize my scent and remember me as a friend.

I had been half aware of gardening sounds from beyond
a boundary wall of decorative concrete blocks. The sound
of digging ceased when I began my overtures to Clarence
and a few moments later a mellow voice but with a nondescript English accent, definitely not local, said, 'Who
are you and what are you doing there?' The voice sounded
curious rather than angry or nervous.

I straightened up. The woman beyond the mesh and
the boundary wall was surely the culprit who had been
throwing slugs into Charlie's garden. She was, as Charlie
had said, a looker. No, I amended my mental note. Not
so much a looker. Her face was pleasing enough in an
ordinary sort of way and what could be seen of her figure
was good, full-breasted and round-hipped. But it was not
just a matter of looks.

Most women, no matter how seductive they may be
when with a lover, also carry within them a neutral being
who can speak or work with a man on equal terms – if
she chooses to do so. There are others who carry the
atmosphere of the bedroom with them and this was a
perfect specimen. Thanks to some indefinable miracle of
body language or pheromones, the windblown disarray

of her dark hair and the faint sweat on her brow suggested the aftermath of a romp between or above the sheets rather than a stint of outdoor labour. I had to blink twice to assure myself that she was wearing jeans and a heavy sweater and not, as had been my first impression, something quite scandalous in lace and ribbons. Even in the garden, her make-up was perfect, and when she pulled off her gardening gloves I saw that her nails were varnished a dark brown to match her lipstick. The colour was unusual but it perfectly complemented the colouring of her dark hair and brown eyes. She knew how to make the most of her powers, this lady.

It took me a second or two to recover my voice, which had unaccountably deserted me. She waited patiently, seeming accustomed to having that effect on men. 'I'm collecting Clarence on behalf of Charlie Hopewell,' I said at last. 'His son's had an accident on holiday and Charlie's gone to help out. He wants me to take care of Clarence for him.'

'Ah.' Robbed of its context it could have been the sigh that follows orgasm. She nodded and smiled a tiny, knowing smile, suggesting strange intimacies. 'I knew about the accident. Walter – Charlie's son – and Helen live two doors the other side. That's why Charlie came to live here when he retired. They leave the key with me when they're away and Helen phoned to ask what was in the mail and to get me to go on keeping an eye on things. I keep Charlie's spare key as well.' She frowned, prettily. 'Charlie usually got me to look after Clarence when they all went away together. He'd leave Clarence in his kennel and run and I'd feed him and take him out for exercise and clean up any doodies.' She stopped and looked at me, obviously expecting an explanation.

'I gathered that there had been some sort of a coldness,' I said.

'Because I accidentally popped a couple of slugs over the wall? He isn't still holding that against me, is he? I forgot which way I was facing and thought that I was

43

throwing them into the field. I explained that to Charlie,' she said, in the tones of one who is grievously misunderstood. 'I'm sorry if he's still holding a grudge. I rather like the old boy. Charlie, I mean. Clarence I can take or leave. A Houdini among dogs, and when he gets out he chases my cat.'

'He doesn't escape from this run, does he?' I asked.

'Not so much since Charlie put the new gate on. More often from the house or the overhead wire.' She lifted her brown eyes for a moment and I looked and saw that what I had taken for a clothes-line, although at high level, had a pulley to slide on it. 'Charlie likes to give Clarence the freedom of the grass when he can.'

It seemed to be a heaven-sent opportunity to pry a little further into Clarence's mishap. 'Perhaps,' I said, 'Charlie felt that he could hardly leave Clarence in your care when you suspected him of chopping off Clarence's tail.'

She blinked at me, managing to turn the tiny reaction into a flutter of eyelashes. Her mouth made an 'O' which seemed to invite a kiss. 'I never suspected him of any such thing. I wouldn't. I like Charlie.' The 'O' had become a complacent smile. 'He flirts outrageously. I told him once that he was too old for that sort of behaviour, but he said that it was hardly his fault that I'd been born about thirty years later than fate intended.'

'Charlie believes that you reported hearing Clarence screaming.'

'Is that all?' She stopped smiling and laughed nervously. 'When the local bobby and the SSPCA man came round, I told them that I'd heard Clarence squealing. Well, it was only the truth, wasn't it? Even Charlie admitted that Clarence had squealed. I wasn't to know whether it was because of having his tail cut off or a tourniquet being put on the wound, which is what Charlie said later had been happening at the time.'

'You couldn't see what was happening?'

'I was indoors. By the time I'd woken up to what I was

hearing and dashed outside, it was all over. Charlie had Clarence in his kitchen and the doors shut. A few minutes later he put Clarence and the girl in his car and they were off to the vet.'

'So you never saw the offcut of tail?' I asked her. She shook her head. 'You don't know whether it was ever found? And you didn't see what direction Clarence came home from?'

'If he really was coming home. No, I didn't.' She came closer and leaned her elbows on the wall and her bosom on her forearms. I tried not to admire too obviously the pair of high-slung spheroids, and wondered how one could know how something would feel just by looking from a distance. 'Look, what is all this?' she asked.

'Charlie's a friend,' I said. 'He swears that Clarence came home with his tail docked and bleeding, but there seem to be some wild accusations flying around. I'd like to get at the truth.'

'Well, I've told you all I know.' She looked at me consideringly. 'I was just going inside for a cup of coffee. Would you care for one? My husband's away just now. I'm Carol, by the way. Carol Haven.'

As an invitation, accompanied by some more eyelash fluttering, it was pretty blatant. It was not an invitation which I was inclined to accept. Although my general health was recovering by leaps and bounds, Beth was still more than enough woman for me to try and keep pace with. And, anyway, I was already due to meet Angus. I thanked her and promised to join her for coffee on some other occasion.

Mrs Haven opened her eyes wide in surprise and turned away. I watched her rear view until the back door hid it from me. Her figure might be a gift of nature, but her walk, which had been perfected after years of practice, was meant to be admired and I saw no reason not to oblige.

When I looked down, Clarence had emerged from his kennel and was nosing my leg in a subdued version of his usual friendly manner and cautiously wagging what was left of his tail. When he looked up at me, it seemed to be knowingly – one dog of the world to another. I slipped the lead round his neck and took him out. He dragged his feet as we neared the gate and then bolted into the back of the car where he seemed soon to be quite at ease with the other dogs.

Clarence would probably settle more happily if he had some familiar object with him – his bedding, perhaps, or a bowl. I went back round the house to the kennel. Mrs Haven was already back at her gardening and did not look up.

I returned to Charlie's front garden carrying a rolled-up dog-mattress of denim cover and polystyrene beads, and found more drama developing. Hannah, Charlie's daughter, key in hand, was heading for her home front door. She was clean and tidy but had made no attempt to glamorize herself. To me, fresh from the hothouse sophistication of Mrs Haven, Hannah's artless youth would have come as a breath of fresh air after a suffocation of deodorant, except that she was moving with the stamping gait of someone in a furious temper and her expression would have stopped a charging mastiff in its tracks.

From the neighbouring house on the further side from the luscious Mrs Haven, an older woman emerged. 'Do come back, you silly child,' she called. There was another face at the window.

Hannah paused and looked round. 'I'm not a child,' she shouted. 'And no way am I coming back. Not with you thinking what you're thinking.'

The woman came out onto the pavement, but stopped when it was clear that Hannah intended to run if she approached any closer. 'I'm sorry, my dear,' she said more softly. 'I didn't mean to upset you. Do come back.' She was a sensible-looking woman in middle age, expensively but unfashionably dressed.

'How dare you tell me to stay away from the Dicksons'

46

dog?' Hannah demanded indignantly. Tears were staining her cheeks. 'I've known Sandy for years. If you think that I hurt Clarence, you must be off your trolley. Clarence is my friend, the only friend I've got.'

'Do please be sensible,' the woman begged. She cast a horrified look around the street, but most of the listening ears were discreetly out of sight. 'You can't possibly stay there on your own. Your father left you with me. What is he going to say if I let you stay alone in that house and try to do your own cooking?'

'I didn't hurt Clarence, whatever you think,' the girl retorted in a choked voice, 'and I'm not coming back with you. I may not be much of a cook, but I can spread things.' Hannah looked wildly around and saw me hovering uncertainly at the corner of the house. For a moment I thought that she was going to bolt for home and shut out the world. But she stood her ground and began to calm down. 'I know you,' she said. 'You're John. You're a friend of Dad's.'

'That's right,' I said.

'Dad was going to ask you to look after Clarence. Did you tell him that you'd do it?'

'Of course. I've just put him in the car.'

Hannah's brow cleared. She smiled. 'You go in for spaniel training. You have lots of dogs, don't you?'

'Oodles,' I said.

'And I remember your wife,' Hannah said. 'Betty, is it?'

'Beth.'

'That's right. Beth. She's nice. She was showing me how to teach Clarence to walk properly at heel and not pull.' She came closer. 'Can I come with Clarence and stay with you and Beth until Daddy gets back? He said that he'd only be away for a few days.'

The woman was looking scandalized and yet at the same time relieved. I wasn't at all sure what Beth would say if I went for a dog and brought back a girl. 'I suppose, if it's all right,' I began weakly.

'It might be the best answer,' said the woman helplessly.

'Once she makes up her mind like this she never changes it. I'm afraid I was a bit ham-fisted.'

I looked at my watch. Angus would be getting up a head of steam by now. 'I have to go and swap cars,' I said. 'I'll be back quite soon. If you're sure that it's what you want, can you pack all that you'll need and be waiting for me?'

Hannah nodded, quite happy. 'I'll be ready,' she said.

'Bring country things mostly. Thick sweaters and welly boots.'

'Give me your phone number,' the woman said to me. 'While you're gone, I'll phone your wife and make sure that it's all right with her.'

'Good idea,' I said. Very sensibly, the woman wanted to check that I really did have a home and a wife and that Hannah would not be destined for the white slave trade. 'Let her know that I'm only helping out in an emergency.' I groped in my pocket for a business card. 'You must be Mrs Turner,' I said.

She nodded briskly. 'Mildred Turner.' She studied my card. 'Oh, you're John Cunningham. Charlie Hopewell's mentioned you.'

For lack of any other answer, I shook her hand before driving off.

THREE

'What on earth was I expected to say?' Beth exploded as soon as Hannah, with Clarence on a lead, was out of earshot. 'A strange woman phones up to ask if it's all right for you to bring Charlie Hopewell's delinquent daughter to stay with us. How could I say, "No, it bloody well isn't. I've more than enough to do already and I don't want somebody around that I have to watch all the time." '

'She isn't that bad,' I said feebly. 'I don't think you can call her delinquent. Whenever I've encountered her she's seemed docile and helpful and perfectly capable of following instructions. It's just that she resents her father's lingering authority and she has a quick temper.' Beth is usually peaceful and accommodating. To meet this resistance from her was a new and sad experience.

Beth produced a glare which, coming from her youthful and gentle face, was as disturbing as a snarl from a china doll. 'You don't know anything about it. So she has a temper. That could mean anything or nothing. She's probably the one who cut off Clarence's tail, and you want to let her loose here, where we have – how many spaniels is it?'

'They're all docked already,' I reminded her. 'And when we discussed it earlier you said that you didn't believe that she did it.'

'I think I said that I didn't want to believe it,' Beth said. 'She might not stop at tails, next time it might be ears or noses or . . . or worse. And it isn't just the dogs. There's Sam.'

49

'Now you're going overboard. She wouldn't touch Sam. She didn't touch Clarence. She's the one person he's completely at ease with. He'd surely react differently if she'd cut off his tail.'

'That at least seemed to be true,' Beth said, although secretly I did not refine too much on it. As soon as he was well away from the scene of the assault on his rear appendage, Clarence had reverted to his real, basic self – a happy and affectionate dog worried only about where the next meal was coming from. He had gone off with Hannah, securely on a lead, while they both explored their new temporary home. But dogs sometimes disbelieve or blame themselves for a single act of cruelty from a beloved owner.

Clarence was also showing a definite tendency to cling close to Hannah and to us, but we were not fooled. The confirmed wanderer dog never reveals any wicked intent, but gives a perfect impression of one who has long outgrown such foolishness; and then suddenly just isn't around any more. But the wanderer will, more often than not, stray from somewhere close to home so that return to the fold, when tired, satisfied or hungry, will be easy. Clarence, moreover, had probably been taught a salutary lesson about the perils of straying. All the same, rather than take any chances, we put him into our most secure accommodation and resolved to walk him only on the lead. This was apparently the regime at home and Hannah accepted it.

Next morning, before the chores were finished, Mrs Turner arrived in a smart little Suzuki. Her conscience must have been pricking at relinquishing Hannah into a stranger's care, because she seemed relieved to find that all was well and that Hannah was contentedly exercising dogs while their runs were cleaned.

I wanted a warm before leaving for Foleyknowe, and Mrs Turner agreed to join me for coffee. I took her into the cluttered, friendly kitchen rather than the more austere sitting room, and she settled happily in one of the basket chairs.

We spoke about Hannah. 'She's not a bad girl, you know,' Mrs Turner said.

I decided to delve deeper. 'My wife's a bit nervous about having her around,' I said. 'You know what young mothers are like.'

Mrs Turner seemed amused. 'Bless you, there's no viciousness in the girl. Quite the reverse, in a way.'

'After all,' I said, 'she was expelled from her school.'

'They asked Mr Hopewell to take her away,' Mrs Turner said gently. 'It isn't quite the same thing. She came across another girl bullying a youngster and she took exception. There was quite a lot of sympathy for her point of view, I believe, but it was felt that quite such direct, physical reprisal was more than could be tolerated. And then, if your wife's been hearing stories about the police being called in . . .'

This was terrible. 'Go on,' I said.

'There was nothing much to it.' Mrs Turner half-smiled, reflectively. 'A local lad made an over-enthusiastic pass at her, one dark night, and found that he'd bitten off quite a lot more than he could chew. There was more shouting than actual bodily harm, but blood had been shed – not much and only by her fingernails – so they were both given a stern warning. The young man is still inclined to jump out of his skin when spoken to suddenly, which is all to the good because everybody except his parents had been expecting him to come a worse cropper, the way he was carrying on.'

As I saw Mrs Turner to her car, I decided that Beth would get only a censored version of the disclosures.

Clarence was not among the dogs loaded into Angus's Land Rover. Given the use of that vehicle (and provided that fresh rain did not make the steeper slopes impassable), I could transport, control and instruct several of our dogs in training without neglecting Angus's chores, but Clarence had not been entrusted to us for training and I judged that he would recover his nerve sooner if kept far away from the site of his unhappy experience, wherever that had been. He might also keep Hannah occupied and out of Beth's hair.

At the last moment, Henry, who had walked over with Isobel, decided to join me. I accepted his company, glad to have a gate-opener and somebody to do some of Angus's work for him while I got on with the real business of the partnership.

We travelled in silence, each busy with his own thoughts, until we had crossed the Tay and were well on our way out of Dundee.

'Do you really intend to find out what happened to Clarence?' Henry asked suddenly.

'That's putting it a bit strongly,' I said. 'I have a feeling that something more is wrong, but I'm not planning to mount an investigation. It isn't my business, it might make enemies and I couldn't do it anyway. But, yes, I would like to know the answer, for our peace of mind, also for Charlie's sake and so that that poor kid won't have to go through life with a huge question-mark hanging over her head. If I get the chance to ask a question or two I'll take it. Even if that doesn't produce any answers, the fact that somebody's asking questions may deter whoever did it from a repeat performance.'

'You hope,' Henry said. 'Fair enough. In that case . . . I've been doing a little thinking – assuming, of course, that the deed wasn't done by one of the family. Charlie Hopewell said that Clarence seemed to be coming back from a generally northward direction?'

'So he said.'

'That makes sense. There's nothing much to the south to attract a dog and Clarence would surely have been seen if he'd come home through the village, girning and dripping blood.'

I began to feel slightly sick. I tend to be sensitive about canine suffering and the picture Henry was conjuring up revolted me. 'If he was losing much blood, he couldn't have come very far,' I said.

'I asked Isobel about that. The blood vessels in the tail aren't very major. He needn't have been losing much blood. It depends how sharp the blade was.'

'According to Charlie, the vet said "sharp".'

'He'd have meant sharp as opposed to Clarence having been caught up in machinery or run over by a train, not razor sharp. You know how your face can bleed when you nick yourself with a razor? When a cut's made with a blunter blade, the capillaries close up and there's a lot less bleeding. Isobel said that you'd have the devil of a job severing a tail-bone with a sharp knife unless you found a joint, which would be difficult with a struggling dog. Isobel said that it would be more a job for a metal-cutter or a pair of pruning snips, something like that. Or a hatchet.'

'You mean, he needn't have bled much and so he could have come quite a long way?'

'Precisely. Or,' Henry corrected himself, 'not precisely precisely. How far is "a long way"? About as long as a piece of string or as far as a drunk can walk before he falls down. We'll move on. If you were a dog, would anything attract you to the fields between Charlie's house and our shoot?'

'Strictly speaking,' I said, 'those fields are part of the shoot. We pay a peppercorn rent for them because they're so utterly useless for holding birds. If we could get on top of the predators we might release a few partridges—'

'Or if there were trees and you could teach partridges to roost in them like any other sensible bird,' Henry put in.

'Failing which,' I said, 'we only bother to include that ground at all because our pheasants sometimes stray there and it helps to stop anybody else going after them before the birds realize that they've made a mistake and wander home again. And very occasionally, if the wind's right, we can turn things round and do a drive in that direction. The stubbles have been ploughed, the rest of it was mown for silage and there isn't a decent hedge anywhere away from the roads. There's damn all to attract a dog, not even any sheep.'

'And nobody could have been working in the fields?'

'Not for any reason that I can think of.'

'That's what I thought,' said Henry. 'And much the same applies to the land across the two roads. But alongside the roads, that's different. You've got hedges and rough banks where a spaniel could have a lovely hunt for rabbits and wandering pheasants. You've got scattered houses and cottages where there might be a bitch in season or a cat to chase—'

'Or unguarded food,' I said, 'bread thrown out for the birds and the universal dustbins.' I was managing to think myself into the mind of a spaniel, a knack which often helped me with training problems. 'Children to play with . . .'

I came to suddenly. I had made the turning off the main road without noticing it and we were running into the village. I took the right-hand fork, which seemed to be heading towards Glamis or Forfar, but which was only posted to 'Milkeerie', a destination of which I had otherwise never heard. 'Thanks, Henry,' I said. 'You've clarified my thinking. Not much on this road, though. One farmhouse, a smallholding . . . and a house I never noticed before,' I added as we passed an old stone villa tucked in between two strips of trees. 'Amazing what you don't see when you're driving. There are rather more dwellings on the other road and some of our regular beaters live there.'

'A rough bunch,' Henry said, 'but good to their dogs. You could do worse than enlist their help.'

I grunted a noncommittal sort of agreement although privately I had my doubts. One or two of the beaters seemed ever ready to lay a stick across a misbehaving dog, whether their own or somebody else's. There had been one or two near-fights arising from such causes and I knew that Angus was in the habit of sending certain men to opposite ends of the beating line for that very reason.

'You've got one thing wrong,' Henry said. 'Pull over.'

I drew up on the verge. 'What?'

We had left the village and where we had stopped the road was on a slight rise. We had a panoramic view of the farmland between the village and the hills. It had turned into one of our better winter days, clear, sharp and calm. Henry pointed to a field in the distance, just below the first hill. 'Sheep,' he said.

He was right. The white dots were sheep. They were hidden from Charlie's back garden by the same rise that we were now on. The driver sees much less of the view than does the passenger; even so, I would have expected to know that they were there – unless, of course, they had only just arrived, which seemed unlikely. 'Bill Finlay's the farmer,' I said. 'He usually spends most of the summer stockpiling hay and silage. Then he buys in stirks in the autumn, fattens them under cover during the winter and sells them in the spring when the price is high. He doesn't usually bother with sheep. Somebody must have offered him a thief's bargain.'

'Does Clarence chase sheep?' Henry asked thoughtfully.

'Not that I know of. He's never shown the least interest in them while he's been near me. But sheep can take fright and farmers can jump to conclusions. Afterwards, the dog isn't around to deny the charge and a strand of wool between the teeth would be all the justification that was needed.'

I put Angus's Land Rover into gear and we jerked into motion.

'What you're saying assumes a bullet,' Henry said. 'But from what the vet said, Clarence's tail wasn't shot off. And I don't see how a farmer could hope to get his hands on an alleged sheep-worrier – which, of course, is why the law empowers him to open fire.'

'I don't think that Bill Finlay has a rifle,' I said, 'but let's assume that he does and that he took a shot at Clarence, didn't give enough forward allowance and nicked or severed his tail.'

'The vet wouldn't describe that as being a cut by a sharp instrument.'

'No,' I conceded. 'But Clarence is soft, even for a

spaniel, and he likes and trusts people. He wouldn't know where the pain came from. He'd go straight to the first person who called him, for succour.'

'I wonder,' Henry said. 'If I were a dog and I suffered a sudden and unexplained pain in the arse, I'd bolt home by the shortest route, avoiding people.'

We had already passed the by-road to Bill Finlay's house, but I could picture him clearly, a youngish man, hard-working but slovenly, not very bright and certainly not one to consider the feelings of other people, let alone animals. The possibility that any of our dogs coming down after a pricked bird might be met with a bullet was frightening. We might have time for a word with him on the way back.

I stopped at the shed and heaved a couple of bags of barley into the back of the Land Rover, refusing Henry's help in deference to his years. For a different reason I discouraged him from taking Angus's ATV. I had seen Henry having fun on it once before and egg production had definitely been down that spring.

Climbing the hill by the route that Angus had taken two days earlier, I could see an equally battered Land Rover in the middle distance. I turned off through an open gate and crossed a stubble field. Duggie McKillop, the tenant farmer on the eastern half of the shoot, was at work replacing some rotted fence-posts, his collie sitting tight nearby. Duggie was a middle-aged man, skinny and creased. For no very clear reason I had got on well with him from the start, perhaps because we had always discussed our plans with him before a shoot and dropped in a brace of birds afterwards. Our strict control of foxes may have helped. Duggie kept sheep and twice had had a lamb decapitated by a fox before its body had even emerged from the mother ewe.

Duggie put down his maul – with relief, I thought – and wiped sweat from his face while greeting Henry and myself. We chatted for a minute about Duggie's setaside plans and the possible use of a flushing bar, damning the

Government and the EEC for their joint folly, before I found an opening.

'The Friday before last,' I said, 'in mid-morning. Did you see a spaniel roaming around loose?'

'One of yours?'

'No,' I said, stung on the raw. 'Definitely not one of ours. It was from the village. Somebody seems to have docked its tail for it.'

Duggie tutted. He took off a moth-eaten old cap and scratched his bald spot. 'Couldn't have seen it that morning,' he said. 'I wasno' here. See, there was a roup on near Errol and the wife and I went wi' Bill Finlay. A dashed waste of time; there was nocht there that I wanted and Bill bought a puckle sheep that I'd no' ha' gi'en tuppence for.'

That, if confirmed, would seem to be that. The sheep had not been around when Clarence lost his tail, and two of the nearest three farmers had been away at the sale. Duggie was ready for a chat, but we tore ourselves away and I nursed the Land Rover up to the crest.

Angus had filled the feed hoppers the day before, but an occasional habit of pheasants is to prefer one particular feeder, emptying it and then either standing around and starving while waiting for it to be refilled or else scattering over the boundary, ignoring a dozen other feeders of identical appearance and contents. While I took two dogs onto the nearest grass for a training session, Henry paid his way by setting off with two carrier bags of feed and, on a thong from his belt, what we referred to as the archbishop – a super-priest or club for dealing with any fox found in a snare.

Giving the dogs a brief rest between exercises, I looked down on the road by which we had arrived. On this side of the road stood Foleyknowe House and two farmhouses, but beyond the road was the house which I had noticed for the first time. Somewhere among a scattering of substantial outbuildings, sparks were flickering; possibly a welder, but more probably from a mechanical grinder. Evidently the buildings were in some kind of industrial use.

The first rule of dog-training is never to prolong it until boredom sets in. Henry had only been waiting at the Land Rover for a minute or two when I returned with my pupils. 'Not a sign of a fox,' he said, 'except for some splashes of feathers that look to be several days old.'

We crossed the saddle. Henry climbed down stiffly to open the gate in the farm boundary and walked ahead to chase the pheasants out of the track. Given an unobstructed run, I coaxed the Land Rover past where Angus had nearly bogged down. I stopped at the second group of feeders and released the other pair of dogs while Henry set off on his patrol again.

The springer spaniel's mission in life is primarily to hunt through rough cover, 'springing' the game. (Retrieving was a later addition to the repertoire.) There is a limit to the training for this vocation that can be given on barren ground, even if supplemented by a rabbit pen and by the ingenious contraptions of skin-clad dummies and catapult rubber that were one of my specialities. The time must come for an introduction to real quarry, but that is the time when lessons may go out of the window and steadiness be forgotten in favour of the heady but unacceptable habit of chasing – a particular hazard with spaniels, which at one moment may be being urged on to hunt and a second later be expected to stop dead when an enticing rabbit bolts from nearby.

There was one long patch of gorse which I knew grew in shallow soil over solid rock and so, although it held rabbits for most of the year, had no bolt-holes. I hunted the dogs one at a time through this, taking the occasional shot as rabbits bolted for holes beyond the open grass, and keeping the whistle handy in case of a failure to 'drop' instantly at the bolting of a rabbit or the flush of a pheasant.

The lesson went well. Ash, who had been sold as a pup and brought back to us for advanced training, showed signs of impetuosity, but got the message after being checked a time or two. After that, progress was rapid and

I might have continued in order to cement the lesson. But movement in the corner of my eye caught my attention. Henry was waving from where the furthest of the feeders stood beside a small stand of silver birch. I drew the session to a close, walked the dogs at heel to the Land Rover and put them away with a word of praise each.

Following one of Angus's fake sheep-tracks that meandered among the bushes, I walked to join Henry. 'Item One,' he said as I arrived. He pointed to the half-buried carcass of a hen pheasant.

'Damn and blast it!' I said, more mildly than I felt. 'If he's put one victim by for another day it strongly suggests that he had at least one other.'

'And I can show you where it is.' Henry led me round the birches to a place where a narrow sheep-track dipped between the nearest tree and some overgrown gorse. 'Items Two A and Two B.'

Item 2A was the corpse of another hen pheasant, this time lying on the surface. Item 2B was the wire snare, originally set close to where the hen lay. This was attached to a concrete block which had now been dragged some yards along the track. The ground between was scored by the marks of a violent struggle.

'We had him,' Henry said, 'and he got away.'

'And now he'll be warier than ever. God bless our legislators,' I added unfairly. So that unintended captures such as badgers or domestic moggies could be released, frightened but unharmed, self-locking snares were made illegal, with the result that a snared fox, instead of dying relatively quickly, may have to wait in the snare twenty-four hours or more; and a side-effect is that a strong fox sometimes manages to free himself from the snare, which surely could never have been the intention.

'Now for Item Three,' Henry said.

'There's more?'

Without immediate answer, Henry led the way over the crest to a strip of gorse running along a steep bank honeycombed with rabbit holes. It was not an area much favoured by pheasants and rather off our beaten track, so that we tended to neglect it. 'You seemed happily occupied,' Henry said, 'so I thought I'd have a poke around and see if there were any other signs. This caught my eye.' He pointed.

Another but smaller wire snare was set from a cut stick in a rabbit-run through the gorse. I walked along a few paces and spotted a second and then a third.

'Would Angus have set those?' Henry asked.

'He never concerns himself with rabbits unless the farmers complain. And they haven't been too bothered this year.'

'That figures. This area's alive with rabbits, but there's nothing in the snares and half a dozen rabbits have been paunched over there,' Henry pointed to the far end of the strip, 'and the guts seem quite fresh and haven't been found by the crows yet, which suggests that the snares have been visited this morning.'

'Which in turn rules Angus out. Well,' I said, 'Angus will have the fellow's guts if he catches him, but it doesn't seem to me that he's doing us a whole lot of harm.'

Henry looked doubtful. 'If he poaches rabbits, will he leave the pheasants alone?'

'If he's after pheasants, would he bother snaring rabbits and risk alerting us? Not everybody has your addiction to pheasant,' I reminded him. 'We have enough to do. We'll let Angus worry about it.'

'Fair enough,' Henry said.

From our fresh vantage point we had a view for miles over a countryside speckled with trees now stripped by winter. To our left we could see over the lower hill to the roofs of the village in the distance and far beyond that to the broad estuary of the Tay. The dam was in the valley between, with a farmhouse and buildings beyond. The road which was entered from the left fork in the village ran past and formed the western boundary of our shoot. It vanished again, in the direction of the unknown Kirkton of Littleknapp, to the right among the Sidlaw Hills, whose lower reaches, here, were lost in forestry plantations once planted for the grants and tax exemptions and now apparently forgotten.

Beyond the road, the Foley Burn, which meandered past the village and thence to the Tay, had cut itself a tree-hung gulley, but on this side of the road and immediately below us was a string of cottages. These had been built (for some forgotten purpose) in two terraces of four, probably of stone but now roughcast. To judge from the back garden walls the group nearer to the village had been converted into two houses of more generous size, with neat gardens given over – as well as I could judge at the distance – to grass and flowers. The other four remained separate, and their gardens were dug over for vegetables and held unmatched sheds.

Beyond the village end of the cottages and across the road I could make out an opening in the trees. The burn must have been bridged because the slated roof of a larger house showed above a screen of evergreens.

'Did somebody say that one of the beaters lives in those cottages?' Henry asked.

'At least one,' I said. 'Bob Somebody. Roberts, that's it. Bob Roberts. The big chap with the beard. But there's another occasional beater. I forget his name. He's what I think they call a Directional Driller on the oil rigs. He gets called away for weeks at a time to ensure that the drill string goes where it's supposed to go, but he comes beating whenever he's on shore when we shoot. I think he lives there.'

Henry nodded twice, once to acknowledge the information and once towards the farmhouse. 'And who's the farmer?'

'Albert Dodd. A crabby old bastard,' I said. I was going to say more, but I realized that I had said all that I had to say about Albert. Quite forgetting about such matters as rent and leases, keepering and the cost of the birds, Albert was convinced that in a just world he would have had the right to shoot the pheasants or share in the profits. This belief resulted in an uneasy relationship, both parties

61

sticking strictly to the letter of their leases and giving no quarter. To be fair, if we agreed to pay him to erect a fence or plant a strip of game-crop, the job would be well and honestly done; but if we were rash enough to consult him about our plans for a shooting day, we were certain to find sheep or cattle or a working tractor just where we least wanted them.

'Yes. I've heard about him. He's not Angus's favourite either,' Henry said.

'His son's all right,' I said. 'He does most of the work. Unfortunately, you can never get hold of him. Or, if you can, Dodd the Father will contradict whatever Dodd the Son told you. There's nothing to be done about it except try to outlive the old devil.'

Descending into the valley again at the western end, the Land Rover was trying to slither on the damp grass. I engaged four-wheel drive and let it choose its own pace.

When the slope levelled off and the Land Rover slowed, Henry opened his eyes, took a deep breath and looked at his watch. 'Are we grabbing an early lunch or making a start on the other side?' he asked.

'Once we climb the other slope, we may as well do the whole job,' I said.

'Then let's have lunch.'

'How would you fancy a short walk first?'

'To raise an appetite? Unnecessary, my appetite is already at its apogee. But why not?'

At the bottom of the field, Henry had to descend to let me through another gate. We skirted the dam, putting ducks into the air – teal and pintail as well as our mallard. The teal usually kept to a far corner, away from the more boisterous mallard. The grain and potatoes scattered around and the small seeds in the shallow margins were appreciated by more than our local stock. There would be more overnight visitors when the duck flew in from daytime roosts; these were our releases plus a lazy few which had taken up residence.

I gave them a blast of the horn to unsettle them. Any fool can raise tame duck, but to raise wild duck takes hard work and a hard heart. Two more gates and a stretch of deeply rutted track and we were near Albert Dodd's farmyard.

There was no sign of the old devil. We left the Land Rover well out of harm's way on a patch of rough ground behind two barns and set off. I carried my gun and took one of the spaniels, on the principle that no chance of a minute's exercise or training should ever be wasted. The field had been drilled with a winter crop; we detoured around the young barley and followed a dense hedge bordering the road, heading away from the direction of the village.

Before we reached the cottages, the field boundary took a bend away from the road. The cottages had been built along one side of a triangle of waste ground, largely a jungle of weeds and bushes but in places a dumping ground for unwanted stones, prams and refrigerators. A path had been worn and in places even maintained, serving the gates in the back garden walls, and we followed the path. My guess was that the back of the cottages would be more revealing than the front. I put the spaniel to hunt. He was another of our pups, sold the previous year and brought back by an impatient owner who had tried to progress too quickly and now wanted me to correct his mistakes. The spaniel put up several pheasants but there were very few rabbits around.

In the middle of a working day, there was little life to be seen around the cottages other than the several cats wandering the gardens or taking what sun was to be had on the shed roofs. They looked without interest at the spaniel, secure in the knowledge that they could outrun or outfight any mere dog. A tall woman with dark grey hair got into a dark grey car at the gable of the first double cottage and drove off as we arrived. The second seemed deserted. The cottages had been built to a commonplace standard, but efforts had been made to upgrade them. As I had guessed, the first garden had been laid out for beauty and leisure by occupiers who

63

were prepared to buy their vegetables. There was cypress hedging to screen a tank for domestic fuel oil. The second garden was different, very neat but given over to herbs and to some plants which were unfamiliar to me.

There was a break before the first of the single cottages, where most of the large back garden was occupied by a complex of sheds. Nobody was in view, but I could hear the sound of somebody sawing timber by hand. Next door, at a cottage where the accommodation had been increased by the addition of dormer windows, the gate was sagging open on a garden that was mostly dug over but still held a few ragged cauliflowers and Brussels sprouts. I could see a fat woman bustling about in a modernized kitchenette.

The two gardens beyond were also empty. I had no excuse prepared for knocking on doors. I was about to give up and turn back when a large, bearded man came out of the back door of the furthest cottage and vanished into another shed. He emerged again a second or two later and set to work.

'Bob Roberts?' Henry whispered.

'Correct.'

Roberts's gate, when we reached it, was ajar. I saw that he had collected a hatchet and, seated on an upturned log, was splitting another into kindling, using unnecessary force so that he sometimes had to drag his hatchet out of the chopping log below. The signs were that the hatchet was very sharp. He seemed impervious to the cold of the day – there was a gap the size and shape of a Rugby football between his jeans and the T-shirt which was all that he wore on his torso. His dog, a Labrador/collie cross, lay nearby but looked at us with cold eyes and gave a single low bark, seeming to imply that that was all that we were worth. Roberts looked up and saw us. He sank his hatchet into his chopping-log, got to his feet and came slowly down the garden. I noticed that his garden was tidier than those of his immediate neighbours.

'You wanted something?' he asked. His accent came

from Dundee itself rather than the Angus countryside.

'Well, Bob,' I said. 'Not working today?'

'Not working any day. Got laid off last month, didn't I?'

'I didn't know that. I'm sorry. You'll be out to beat for us on Saturday, then?'

'Did I ever let you down? Now you tell me. Are we having a Keeper's Day this January? That bugger Todd wouldn't promise.'

I could almost have smiled. It was a debate which had maddened Angus, but I found it rather funny. The Keeper's Day, traditionally the last shooting day of the season and one to which usually only the beaters and pickers-up are invited, is a valued perk. But the beaters know how to drive the ground better than the host and often better even than the keeper. In the previous January, our beaters had divided themselves into three teams standing in turn, leapfrogging each other in two Subaru pick-ups so that at any given moment there was one group standing to shoot, one group beating towards the first and the third probably already in transit. Ignoring Angus's attempts to call for moderation, they had managed fourteen drives in the day (as against the six to eight which was our norm) and had so nearly cleared the ground that Angus had been hard put to it to catch up the birds that he needed for his intensive rearing programme. Another result was that we had fewer wild clutches than usual this year – but very little difficulty recruiting beaters.

After endless debate we had decided on a compromise only a few days earlier. 'You'll get two days instead of one,' I said. 'But cocks only. Anyone shooting a hen goes straight home and doesn't come again.'

He knew what I meant. Any cock pheasants left wild at the end of the season, over and above the minimum number required for breeding, were consumers of expensive feed and, worse, by squabbling over and pestering the available hens they worsened the prospect of broods raised in the wild to supplement the released birds.

'Right,' said Roberts. He was not a man to make concessions to anybody. If anything, he looked slightly put out at having been robbed of a valued grievance. There would be no point making subtle approaches.

'Somebody's snaring rabbits on the shoot,' I said. 'I don't grudge him a few rabbits but I'd like to know who it is.'

'It isn't me.'

I believed him. Roberts's style would have been to take his gun and his dog and shoot the rabbits, daring Albert Dodd or Angus to do something about it. 'I never thought that it was,' I said. 'But do you know who it is?'

He shook his head. There was no expression on his beard but I was sure that he knew. There was no point pursuing it. That sort of loyalty between neighbours is seldom breached. 'You know Charlie Hopewell?' I asked.

Bob Roberts nodded. 'From the village.' He scowled. 'Bloody tyke of a spaniel. Comes round here raising hell.'

'Did the dog come round here a week past last Friday?' I asked. 'That was the day of the rainstorm.'

'Why do you want to know?'

I tried not to sigh. Bob Roberts, I recalled, was an efficient beater but on his own terms. Angus might give out orders, but Roberts would do the job in what he believed to be the best way. As far as he was concerned, he was always the one in step. 'On that Friday morning,' I said, 'he strayed from home. When he returned, some-body had chopped off half his tail.'

Roberts's face did not change, so far as I could tell, behind the beard, but he said, 'That's nasty. You think he came this way?'

'It seems possible,' Henry said.

By reputation, Bob Roberts cared more for dogs than for people, a preference for which I had some sympathy. The news brought on a rare burst of speech. 'Could be. I didn't see him, but he came this way often enough. The widow woman at the far end, Mrs Bell, chased him away with a stick once for messing on her lawn; she was home that Friday, if I mind right. I saw her pruning her rose-bushes before the rain. And then there's Jim O'Toole.

He's aye here, for he runs a cabinet-making and repair business from his shed. He and his missis have a miniature poodle bitch as is in season just now.' He paused and stooped to pull the ears of my spaniel, but his loquacity had not quite run out. 'I can see why you're fashing yoursel'. You think somebody may have it in for spaniels? Or for dogs in general? Or for Mr Hopewell?'

'None of those, I hope,' I said. 'But I'd like to be sure. Do you have any suggestions?'

He dried up immediately. 'No,' was his sole reply.

He was not a man to be pushed. Perhaps he could be led to open up a bit. 'Do you know the Hopewell lassie?' I asked him.

He scowled, his first visible expression. 'Don't you go suggesting any such thing. Yon lassie may not be college material but she's good wi' dogs. And she's a fine girl. Just fine,' he repeated. 'There's naethin' adae wi' her. And at least she has enough sense to chase the village lads away, which is more than you can say for some.'

'I'm inclined to agree. If you think of anything, let me know,' I said. Before turning away, I added, 'I hope you get fixed up soon. Why don't you go offshore?'

His beard sneered at me. 'Not much call for foresters on the rigs,' he said. 'That's what I was, up-bye.' He nodded towards the regimented lines of spruce which began beyond the first crest. 'The estate's cutting back. I could get work if I moved, but why should I? I'm settled here. The Government changed the rules, about taxes and subsidies and the like of that. Let the bastards keep me for a change, out of the money they saved.'

As if that was quite enough talk for one day, he turned his back without another word and set off up the garden.

We returned by the path along the garden walls. The spaniel put up a pheasant, but we were still too near the dwellings even for a shot in the air. Just beyond the cottages, Henry stopped suddenly. A tumble-drier had been discarded and was lying on its side, rusting away and Henry pointed at it.

'They'd probably be only too pleased if you took it with

you,' I said. Henry ties flies for his trout fishing, and copper wire from electric motors is always in demand. But he shook his head in annoyance and pointed out a vertical line of spots on the white enamel which could have been blood.

'Wouldn't the rain have washed it off?' I asked.

'That storm came from the east,' Henry said. 'This side would have been sheltered. But I don't see how a dog with a severed tail could make a vertical line of spots.'

'Perhaps it was standing upright at the time and it's been knocked over since,' I suggested. But when we moved the white box-shape it was obvious from the long-dead grass beneath that it had lain where it was for some time.

Henry gasped suddenly. 'Take another look,' he said.

When I looked I saw that there were more and fresher lines of droplets. Henry showed me his palm. There was a clean but shallow cut welling blood. We found a sharp sliver of metal at a corner of the tumble-drier. Some other person or animal had fallen foul of it.

I rolled the dead machine over so that the razor-edge of steel was in the ground. It would soon rust away. 'Come on back to the Land Rover,' I said. 'Angus keeps a first-aid box, mostly for any dog that gashes itself on barbed wire, but also for beaters who get peppered. I'll put a dressing on it. Try not to get blood on your clothes.'

The spaniel was back in the Land Rover, I had applied some antiseptic to Henry's wound and was adding a plaster from Angus's ample stock when Dodd the Father made his appearance. He was a small man, gaunt and wiry, of any age from fifty upwards, who always looked as though he had grown straight out of the ground, clothes and all. He launched straight into the usual tirade. Sheep had been frightened, gates left open, crops trodden underfoot, electric fences switched off, other fences broken down, litter deposited, fires started, vegetables stolen.

None of it was true. Some of it would have been impossible at that season. I let him rant while I attended to Henry. When he had got it out of his system I said, 'Do you ever see a spaniel wandering loose around here?'

He looked at me hard, wondering which answer would annoy me more. 'Now and again,' he said cautiously.

'When you do, what do you do about it?'

'I haven't seen one for months.' His response was immediate, instinctive and could have been true or false.

I decided to follow a different line. 'Have you given anybody permission to take rabbits?'

'What if I have? I'm allowed to control vermin.'

'You know that your lease requires you to notify me of any such permissions. You haven't done it, so if he poaches pheasants you're liable for the cost.'

He thought my bluff over and changed tacks. 'There's nobody has my leave to take rabbits. You're supposed to be keeping them down and you're no' doing it. They're eating me out of business.'

'Last time I wanted to organize a rabbit-shoot, you said you liked to have them around,' I reminded him. I was about to climb into the driver's seat and leave him gobbling, when another question occurred to me. 'Almost opposite your road-end, there's a driveway and a bridge to a house among the trees. Who lives there?' I asked.

He grinned at me, gap-toothed. 'Nearn House? That'll be Mr Ricketts. A fine gentleman. You should pay him a call. You'd deal well together, the pair of you.'

He plodded off towards the house without another word. I turned the Land Rover and set off after him. There was a wet patch where I thought that I might be able to spray him with mud as I went by – accidentally, of course. But he was already past it when I arrived. I drove on, consoling myself with the thought that a little more mud on him would never have been noticed.

FOUR

Time had slipped away from us and the lunch-hour was now well advanced. The hotel bar, when we entered it, contained a mixed throng of lunchers and drinkers. We pushed through to the bar counter, for beer and to order our lunches.

Henry took a look around. 'Isn't that the woman who was driving off from the cottages as we got there?' he asked.

I followed his eyes. He was looking at a thin woman in her forties who was sitting alone, eating a salad at a corner table. Her neatly styled hair, which had been allowed to go grey, looked familiar. 'I think you're right,' I said. 'Go and grab the table next to her. What do you want to eat?'

'The steak pie,' Henry said over his shoulder. He was already on his way. He just beat a young couple with a child to the table we wanted. They found another table and sat glaring at Henry.

Our beers came. I ordered our meals and paid for the lot – Henry was never paid for his services but by tacit agreement he was our guest whenever he lent a hand. I carried his lager and my Guinness over. Henry had already drawn the woman into conversation, and although her intelligent features could have been severe, I saw that she was smiling. Henry might have left his boyhood far behind him but his boyish charm had weathered well. I sat down opposite Henry in the chair nearest to the lady.

'I wasn't mistaken,' Henry said. 'This is Mrs Bell. John Cunningham,' he added in her direction.

70

We said that we were pleased to meet each other. Mrs Bell was smartly but modestly dressed. At first glance I would have put her down as one of those acidulous females who can be counted on to disapprove of everybody and everything except their own immediate relatives, but when I looked again her smile had a humorous twist matched by an amused glint in her eye.

'We saw you drive off as we walked past your house, about an hour ago,' I said.

'So Mr Kitts told me, by way of an introduction. I've seen you before, too.'

'Really?'

'Yes. I was taking some bulbs from my garden to a friend of mine in the village, yesterday. Her next-door neighbour's daughter was kicking up a fuss and you stepped in, like a knight in shining armour. You'll have to be more careful about your tendency to knight errantry or the girl will fall for you.'

I hoped that she was joking. But without knowing it she had given me a valuable opening. 'Your friend wouldn't be Mrs Haven?' I asked.

'Certainly not!' She looked disapproving but only mildly so. 'The other side. Mildred Turner, the lady that the Hopewell girl was supposed to stay with. You know that Mr Hopewell's abroad just now, of course. Some accident to his son, I believe.'

'A broken leg, skiing,' Henry said. 'John had already agreed to look after Charlie's spaniel, Clarence, for him while he's away bringing the invalid home.' He gave me a meaningful look.

I grabbed up the opportunity which Henry had handed me. 'I have a kennels and my partner's a vet,' I said. 'Charlie particularly wanted Clarence to be well cared for. Did you know that somebody chopped off part of Clarence's tail about ten days ago?'

The waitress arrived with Henry's steak pie and my lemon sole. 'I knew something, but no details,' Mrs Bell said when our food had been safely delivered and the waitress had finished trying to be a little mother to us. 'And I certainly saw Clarence going around with his tail in a sling – metaphorically speaking,' she added quickly in case we should not realize that she was joking. 'If you're who I think you are, you operate the Foleyknowe shoot. Am I right?'

'Quite right,' I said.

I prepared myself for the usual female blind assumption that shooting must *ipso facto* be cruel, but no such thought was in Mrs Bell's mind. 'I can see why you might be worried,' she said. 'All those dogs running loose. What do you suppose did happen to Clarence?'

'I'm spending my odd spare moments trying to find out,' I said. 'At present, we don't even know where. It seems possible that he may have gone visiting in your direction. Were you at home in the morning, a week past Friday? The day of the rain?'

'Yes,' she said without hesitation. 'Until mid-morning.'

Most people, if asked what they were doing even a couple of days before, hum and haw and look in their engagement diaries unless something very significant happened on that day. Mrs Bell must have caught my speculative glance in her direction.

'I'm at home every Friday morning,' she explained. 'It's the day the butcher's van comes round. He's a surly devil but he carries good meat. That's the one shopping facility that we most miss in the village. So I stay at home on Fridays and do my gardening and cleaning and laundry. Other days, I finish up by mid-morning and walk or drive into the village to do a little shopping and visiting. Usually I have lunch with Mildred Turner or she comes back with me. Today, she's got visitors and the visitors have children and I do think that hell must be crowded with other people's children. I didn't fancy lunching alone in an empty house – I've had enough of that since my husband died. So I came here.'

'If you remember that Friday—' I began.

Henry interrupted me. 'John is about to ask you

72

whether you saw or heard Clarence near your home. But, thinking it over, I've realized that Clarence must have lost his tail somewhere more isolated or the noise he'd have made would have been heard by everybody for miles around.'

'Not necessarily,' I said. 'Nature has it well figured out. For as long as the attack continues, a dog will give tongue, but a dog that's been peppered, for instance, doesn't always start yelping until some minutes later. Just as a soldier who stops a bullet doesn't always feel the pain right away. Nature gives you time to get out of harm's way and, while you're running off, a lot of noise would only draw some more hostile attention to you.'

'You should know,' Henry said. 'John was an army captain. Served in the Falklands.'

'Well, you may both be perfectly correct,' Mrs Bell said. 'I'm sure you are. But Clarence could have squealed his head off and nobody would have heard him. Mr O'Toole, who does cabinet-making and furniture repairs in the sheds behind his cottage, was cutting up his new stock of hardwoods and putting it by to season. His big saw makes such a noise that you can't hear yourself think. I didn't even hear the butcher's van arrive, although he always sounds his horn. When he was due, I looked out of the window to see what was keeping him, and there he was, waiting, not very patiently as it turned out.

'Mr O'Toole doesn't use the big saw very often, thank God! I'll say that much for him. About three times a year, I suppose. If it was any oftener, I'd move away. But when he does use it, frankly, you couldn't hear a bomb go off. The rest of the time, he's merely a bloody nuisance, if you'll pardon my French. He had already driven me indoors out of the garden, but the rain was obviously coming anyway. So as soon as the butcher had been, which was about eleven-thirty, I decided to forget about the hoovering, leave the washing-machine running and come down to visit Mildred for a little peace and quiet. So I can't honestly claim to have seen or heard anything that day. And I don't hold out too much hope of any of the others.'

Mrs Bell had finished her meal and with it what looked like a half-pint of shandy. I offered her another drink but she shook her head. 'I'd be running out all afternoon, thank you very much,' she said frankly, not quite laughing at me. 'But I'll take a cup of coffee, if you're on a spending spree.'

'I'll get it,' Henry said, rising.

'Plain milk and no sugar, please.'

Henry headed in the direction of the tea and coffee dispensers at the end of the bar counter.

'Did you drive straight to Mildred's house that day?' I asked.

'Yes. Why?'

'I think you'll see,' I said. 'Were you there before Clarence's return?'

She smiled again. Her smile sat lightly on her severe features. 'I think it was almost a dead heat. I could hear some yelping as I got out of the car and Mildred said something about Clarence seeming to have hurt himself.'

'That's very interesting,' I said. 'Which would you expect to do the journey more quickly, you driving or Clarence on foot?'

Mrs Bell laughed. 'I may not be that laddie Damon Hill, but I'll back myself against Clarence any day of the week.'

'So if Clarence got himself pruned in your neighbourhood, it must have been round about the time of the butcher's van?'

She gave it some thought, not smiling. Now and again she reminded me of a stern headmistress from my infant days, but moments later she might be alight with mischief. I thought that she must have been a hell of a girl in her day. 'I'd say that that was about right. Certainly no later. But that's rather a big if. The rain was fairly rattling down, so nobody was out for walkies. On the other hand, one does look out of the window now and again and we had

74

to go out to visit the van-driver. Anybody moving around outdoors in the pouring rain is apt to attract attention.'

'That's true,' I said.

'I remember the Hopewell girl going by on her bicycle while I was at the butcher's van, soaking wet and dashing for home. And there was a yellow car going the other way. I think that's all.' She paused and gave me a sudden glance which was disconcertingly intense. 'I can understand your interest. But why aren't you leaving it to the SSPCA? Or the police?'

'From what Charlie Hopewell told me,' I said, 'some of his neighbours have been putting in the poison. They seem to have given the authorities reason to believe that Charlie may have docked his own dog's tail.'

'Rubbish! I believe he'd kill anyone who laid a finger—' she stopped abruptly.

'That's pretty much what I said,' I told her. 'Between ourselves, I think he's afraid that his daughter may be blamed. So afraid that he's scared to say it aloud.'

'That's just as silly,' she said stoutly. 'I've met the girl at Mildred's house a dozen times. She's temperamental but there's no cruelty in her. At her age, I believe I was a greater rebel against authority.'

'It doesn't sound very likely,' I agreed. 'But the authorities must be used to all kinds of inexplicable behaviour towards animals. They may be envisaging either Charlie or his daughter taking a swipe at Clarence in a fit of temper, breaking his tail and then chopping it off to cover up the deed. Suppose, for instance, that Clarence snapped at a biscuit and gave Hannah a nip in the process?'

'Well,' said Mrs Bell indignantly, 'I still wouldn't believe it and the authorities certainly didn't get any such ideas from Mildred or from me. It must have been that flighty young woman on the other side. Pure invention, of course. Charlie Hopewell dotes on that dog and patience is his middle name. Not literally, you understand?' It seemed to be her habit to use imaginative figures of speech and then worry about being taken literally.

'Yes, of course,' I said, laughing.

'That sounded silly, but I wouldn't want you to think that he had a girl's name,' Mrs Bell said, laughing gently at herself. 'Hannah's very good with domestic animals. And Charlie's been more patient with Clarence than most owners would have been.'

'In what way?'

'We've watched. The side-window of Mildred's sitting room looks that way and it catches the sun, so we often sit there. Most men would have given up, had Clarence neutered or put down. But no. At first, Clarence only ran off when he was loose, so Mr Hopewell took to keeping him on the lead. Next, he went over the top of the run from the roof of his kennel. So Mr Hopewell made it higher and higher until not even Clarence could go that high. And he had to reinforce the gate. He said to Mildred once that if he'd known that he was going to spend his retirement building Colditz for a spaniel he'd have stayed in business. Next thing, Clarence dug under the wire and Mr Hopewell had to mix a whole lot of concrete. He and Hannah did it between them.

'That stopped Clarence getting out of the pen. But Mr Hopewell must have felt sorry for the dog, cooped up in a kennel and a concrete run all day except when he was being walked on a lead or at work. So he takes Clarence into the house whenever he can although Clarence can nose open a window and I'm sure that he can also work the lever handle of any door that opens away from him. And Charlie strung a high wire across the garden, like a washing-line ... Thank you,' she added to Henry, who had returned with three coffees.

'I saw it,' I said. 'I thought at first that it really was a washing-line.'

'Mr Hopewell sends everything to the laundry. He says that if he was still working he could find time for doing the washing but retirement time is too precious to waste. No, he put that wire up specially. At first he just had the ring sliding on it and attached to a sort of long dog-lead, so that Clarence had access to the patio and most of the lawn, but Clarence soon learned to shake his head until the loop of chain slipped off. Leather collars are no good on Clarence – unless they're tight enough to strangle him he just pulls until they come off over his head. We've watched it all happening, a sort of duel of wits, wondering who would win the next round. Next, Mr Hopewell hooked on one of those extending dog-leads. With the other end looped round Clarence's neck, the pull of the spring should have been just enough to prevent the loop of chain falling slack.' Mrs Bell grinned in delighted recollection. 'It took Clarence just two days to beat that one. He pulled out a length of lead, walked three times round one of the posts and *then* shook the chain loop off over his head.'

As I laughed, I was thinking that dogs are not noted for reasoning ability, spaniels come low in the league table and show-bred spaniels very near the bottom. If Clarence was an intelligent mutation, perhaps we should get a service or two. The habit of wandering may be partly hereditary but it can usually be averted by the right training.

'Your friend Mildred didn't have any trouble with Clarence?' I asked.

'Losh no! Or if she did it was her own fault. She thinks he's perfect. She gives him biscuits whenever he comes visiting. I'd be more likely than she would to take a swipe at the perisher.'

Mildred, I decided, was the one who needed something painful in the vicinity of the backside. I had the strongest objection to neighbours who encouraged my dogs to stray, unbalanced their diets and made them fat.

Mrs Bell was clearly one of those perfect informants, a born gossip, and I wanted to exploit her for all she was worth. 'And the lady the other side?' I enquired.

She raised her eyebrows, simulating amazement. 'Smile when you call her a lady or folk may think that you're serious. Mrs Postman Pat—'

'Who?'

'Mrs Haven. Her husband's a postman in Dundee and his first name is Pat. And he really does look a bit like the children's character, tall and thin with a blob for a nose. So naturally everybody calls him Postman Pat – except for those of us who call him Postman Prat, because he does have an exaggerated opinion of himself.'

Henry had been listening keenly but in silence. Now he was struck by the very point I had made to Charlie. 'Rather an expensive area for a postman, isn't it? New bungalows in exclusive cul-de-sacs aren't exactly given away.'

'I suppose it is,' Mrs Bell said. 'They only moved here a couple of years ago and I think he'd come down in the world, got a golden handshake or industrial compensation or something. She hinted that he was only working as a postman to keep himself occupied and his card stamped. But I really can't bring myself to believe a word she says. She flaunts her body, flirts with every male between fourteen and seventy. When my husband was alive, she made advances to him every time they met. I didn't really mind. All that she achieved was to light his fuse for me. And on most days, Mildred says, she disappears for an hour or two in her hideous little yellow car, so there's probably a boyfriend somewhere. They have two cars, on a postman's wage, would you believe? Not brand-new cars, but not very old either.'

Mrs Haven might be an interesting topic but we were straying from the point. Also Mrs Bell, despite her pretence at tolerance, was becoming heated.

'Did she hold a grudge against Clarence for chasing her cat?'

'I don't think she gives a damn for any animal except herself, not even her own cat,' Mrs Bell said. She sniffed. 'She used to feed Clarence for Charlie Hopewell sometimes, but I'm sure that that was just to curry favour with a man. The nearest she came to showing an attitude to the dog was when he chased Mrs Brightley's cat up a chimney and the fire brigade had to get it down again. Mildred saw her actually pat Clarence after that, once.

'I don't think that she'd have hurt Clarence. In fact, I'm surprised to hear that she was even at home at the time. Of course, Postman Pat might have been driving her car,' Mrs Bell said obscurely. 'I'd be more inclined to suspect the policeman in the house the other side of her of *severus dorsus canis* or whatever jargon the lawyers dream up for the offence.'

I pricked up my ears. 'Would that be the policeman who came round with the SSPCA man?' I asked her. From Charlie's viewpoint, it would be useful if the investigating officer could be shown to have a motive for bias.

Her eyes widened. 'I shouldn't think so for a moment. He's much too senior to be bothered with a little thing like an assault on a spaniel's tail. But he's very keen on his garden. He puts into it all the time and energy he can spare from solving murders and treason and company frauds, and more money than I could ever get out of Fred for the garden; and to do him justice, it's becoming a showpiece. But he will put bone-meal round his roses so, of course, Clarence thinks there's a bone buried beneath and he digs them up. Before now, I've heard Detective Chief Inspector McStraun with my own ears, threatening to take his hedge-clippers to Clarence. And not to his tail, either.'

I looked at Henry in surprise, to find that he was looking at me. We had met Detective Chief Inspector McStraun once before when the Tayside and the Fife constabularies had been collaborating on a murder case which had roots in both areas. He had seemed to be a placid man, not given to threats or to outbursts of temper. But at that time he had been on duty. Hell, I knew only too well, has no fury like a passionate gardener whose roses are being uprooted by a neighbour's dog.

'This is very helpful,' I said. 'You're making the locals come alive for me. I don't know whether it'll help to solve the Mystery of the Mad Dog-Docker, or whether that mystery will ever be solved, but I feel I've got to try.'

The humour left her face. 'I think you must,' she said. 'It was a beastly thing to happen. I can do without Clarence treating my garden as a dog's toilet, but I wouldn't do a thing like that to him. I don't have a dog just now. My Shetland collie had to be put down last April – he was sixteen, poor old chap – and I haven't had the heart to replace him yet, but if somebody had maimed him in that sort of way I'd never have rested until I'd done something really horrible to them. And, you're right, the police won't bother, not unless it turns into an epidemic like those cases of horse-slashing.'

I gave an inward shudder. If it turned into an epidemic, my dogs, some of which spent hours working in the area, often out of my sight, would certainly be in the high-risk category. 'Thank you,' I said. 'It seems quite possible that whatever took place happened out in your direction. So who lives in your neck of the woods?'

'All right,' she said. She gave me another of her surprising smiles. 'I don't get very many chances to talk about my neighbours and be thanked for it. You've seen the layout. Starting from the far end there's the big man with the beard.'

'Roberts,' I said. 'I know him.'

'He's another surly devil, but I suppose you can't blame him – he's unemployed, so he's at home most of every day. His wife goes out; I believe she's a hairdresser or some such thing. Role reversal doesn't suit him. I think he feels his masculinity is threatened.'

'No children?' Henry asked.

'Those cottages are mostly too small to raise a family in, although I suppose it would be possible in the one where they've put in dormer windows to make a spare room upstairs. And, of course, at my end two houses have been made out of four cottages. But in fact there isn't a child in the whole row. Isn't that odd? And satisfactory! It must be something in the water. Perhaps we should bottle it.

'Next door to Roberts there's a retired couple, Brora by name. They're struggling along on a pension, but they manage to keep an old rattletrap of a van and they go off most days to visit one or another of their daughters. I'm sure they were away that day, because I remember turning away from the butcher's van under my umbrella and not seeing the Broras' van backed into their front garden.

'Next there's a younger couple, Strichen or Strachan or possibly Buchan. He goes off for weeks at a time to some mysterious job in the oil industry while she cleans and polishes their cottage within an inch of its life, if you can call that living. She was at home that day because she came out to the butcher's van almost on my heels and asked me what the weather was going to do, of all the silly questions. It was raining hard and it was going to go on raining, anybody could have seen that. She's afraid of dogs in general and Clarence in particular.'

'I don't think the name's Buchan,' I said. 'And he's a directional driller.'

'I didn't know that – whatever a directional driller may happen to be. Clarence strolled into their house once and I never heard such a hullabaloo.

'Then comes Mr O'Toole. He's as Irish as his name, been in this country for half a century and still sounds as if he's up to his knees in a peat-bog. His wife sounds local. They're old but they're as tough as old boots; when he's cutting up timber, as he was that day, she gives him a hand and the two of them handle big slabs of hardwood as though they were polystyrene.

'He does beautiful work, repairing damage to furniture of any period or matching up a missing chair from a set. He'd be a pleasure to have around if he wasn't so *berluddy* noisy,' Mrs Bell said, letting her refinement slip for a moment. 'And if I dare to speak to him about it, all I get is an earful of Irish abuse and I can't even answer him back because I didn't understand a word of what he said in the first place. The rest of the time, they're a sweet old couple. I've tried complaining to the Local Authority, but it seems that planning consent slipped through, almost by accident, and there's not a lot they can do about it.'

'They have a bitch in season just now, we're told,' said Henry.

'The miniature poodle with some outlandish Irish name? Is she on heat? I wouldn't know. If Clarence made improper advances, the O'Tooles would cut off more than his tail. They adore that little squeaky toy. I can't imagine why. It isn't as if it's of any possible use, except perhaps as a dish-mop.

'That leaves our next-door neighbours. Bassett by name, and somehow they look it – long and mournful faces, both of them, and soulful eyes. They have a health-food and herbal-medicine shop in Dundee which takes one or both of them away every weekday.'

'Their garden!' I said. 'I thought that it looked different. I suppose those are herbs?'

Mrs Bell was nodding. 'And if Clarence dug up any of those specimens they might well have gone after him with a sharp spade, but I'm fairly sure that neither of them was at home. On top of being cranks, they're religious; and not sensible Protestants, which would hardly count, but one of these freaky religions like Christian Science or Born Again Adventists or I don't know what. And they thoroughly disapprove of you,' Mrs Bell added cheerfully. 'If either of them happens to be at home when you're shooting, they stamp around muttering about sadism and the privileged classes.

'Then there's me. I've certainly shouted at Clarence for coming in and messing up my lawn and then scratching up the turf; and I've no alibi at all until after the butcher's van came. I was in the garden, pruning roses, until the noise drove me indoors, shortly before the thunder-plump started.'

'You were seen,' I told her. 'Roberts confirms seeing you at your roses.'

'Nice of him. Not that it helps. Clarence might have come into my garden and lifted his leg against my favourite ornament while I had the pruning snips in my hand. For all you know, his tail may be buried in my compost heap. Or have you dug it up?'

I assured her that her compost heap was still inviolate.

'A pity,' she said. 'It's overdue for turning. After the rain started, I got most of the carpets hoovered by the time the butcher's van showed up.'

Mrs Bell fell silent and finished her coffee. She seemed to feel that her tale was told.

'There's one more,' I said. 'Across the road and the burn from you and rather nearer the village. Nearn House.'

Mrs Bell lost her air of tolerant amusement and became schoolmistressy again. 'Oh dear!' she said. 'I was hoping that you weren't including that man, whatever his name is, among my neighbours.'

'His name's Ricketts,' I said.

'So it is. He's one person who would almost certainly have been at home,' Mrs Bell said. 'He hardly ever goes out at all except, now and again, he'll walk in here and drink himself stupid. I believe that he gets most of his food and everything else delivered from Dundee. There's one small van in particular that calls almost every day, plus several others that come weekly.

'I do try to be tolerant. I try not to hold it against somebody who's coloured or who has strange beliefs. In theory, I'm even tolerant about strange sexual preferences, as long as they aren't too public about it . . . "and frighten the horses", as somebody said. But sometimes you can't help getting a mental picture of what you think, perhaps quite wrongly, they're up to, and you get the shivers.'

I remembered the relish with which Dodd the Father had suggested that Mr Ricketts and I might get on together and I decided to put the boot in, the next time that the old devil broke the strict terms of his tenancy. 'A bit peculiar, is he?' I asked. I have come to resent the theft of words such as 'gay' from the English language.

'He doesn't ram it down your throat,' Mrs Bell said, and hurried on without seeming aware that she had used a most unfortunate expression. 'In fact, it's a matter of argument locally, whether or not he is homosexual. There doesn't seem to be any real evidence either way. General opinion is that he's as queer as a rubber carving-knife, and he doesn't go out of his way to correct the impression. On the other hand, I remember another man who wore his hair as long and wore the same sort of bright colours and soft fabrics. In that instance, I think that it was just sheep's clothing, because he fathered several children on the wrong side of various blankets, to my certain knowledge. I'm not so sure about Mr Ricketts.'

'Why not?'

Mrs Bell frowned in thought. 'Most people respond more to one sex than to the other. Usually but not always to the opposite sex to their own – it can surprise you, sometimes, if you watch the unlikeliest people. Little things that show up in body language and tone of voice. Mr Ricketts doesn't seem to react to women but he seems to me to be just as neutral with other men.

'I'm told that the inside of the house is decorated like a Turkish brothel. Mrs Strichen or Strachan told me, although how she knows what a Turkish brothel looks like is uncertain. But perhaps I'm not being fair,' Mrs Bell said charitably. 'I believe that she met her husband somewhere abroad. She used to clean Nearn House for Mr Ricketts, one afternoon a week. She says that she's sure there were drugs in the place.

'He never has any guests. If there's anybody in his life it must be somebody local, because someone in a raincoat and a wide-brimmed hat has been seen to visit him on foot – usually at night but sometimes in the mornings, of all the times for that sort of carry-on! I've never seen him myself, but there's a path along the Foley Burn, starting from between the two shops, where there's a way through to some public toilets. Mrs Postman Prat swears that she almost bumped into a man who had his face hidden. Occasionally you can see torchlight bobbing along there after dark, but it could be a dog-walker.'

Mrs Bell's voice faded. She looked around the bar, still half full from the lunchtime throng. I thought that she was probably wondering which, if any, of the locals might be the visiting lover.

Her words had brought a picture to my mind, of a man in white trousers and a shirt the colour of a bad bruise. 'This Ricketts,' I said. 'Is he thin and sandy-haired with a wispy moustache and a defiant look, as though ready to bite?'

'Not just ready but expecting to bite,' she said. 'That's the man.'

'I've seen him in here. He was drinking malt whisky by the double and flashing his money. He offered to buy drinks for anybody but got remarkably few takers. In fact, I noticed one couple turn in the doorway and go out again when they saw who was here.'

'It's a lonely life, being different,' said Mrs Bell.

To the south of the two valleys which formed the centre-piece of the shoot ran a ridge, a last wrinkle of the Sidlaw Hills before the sedimentary plain. More feeders were spread along the ridge and had to be checked and where necessary refilled.

With no snares to be visited on that side of the shoot we might have finished our visits in short time, but I was making the most of the training opportunities afforded by the terrain, the abundant rabbits and the availability of Henry to shoot while I worked the dogs. It was after four and dusk was advancing when we came rattling up the drive at Three Oaks, cold and somewhat weary.

Although I was pleasantly conscious of a day well spent, I was apprehensive. Beth had somehow planted in my mind an irrational idea that Hannah might at any moment give way to an explosion of temper and run riot with whatever weapon came to hand. My guns and my new

85

chainsaw were securely under lock and key, but I was uneasily aware that knives and matches and so-called 'blunt instruments' abounded. I knew that the very idea was nonsense, yet it came almost as a relief to see that the place was still standing and to recognize first Beth's and then Isobel's figures about the place. Beth, who had just emerged from the kitchen door with a trolley of dog food, came to greet us.

'Everything all right?' I asked her.

She looked surprised. 'Yes. Of course.'

'Where's Hannah?'

Beth glanced at the dormer windows and lowered her voice. 'I sent her to have a bath. She really has been working herself to the bone. I'm amazed. She doesn't mind clearing up dog shit. She's terribly good with the dogs and they seem to take to her. She looked around the place for herself and asked if she could move into Daffy's old room behind the kitchen instead of our spare bedroom. She liked the pop-star posters.'

'And Sam?'

Beth's face seemed to change gear and she lowered her voice further. 'She fell for Sam and he seems to like her, but I didn't feel that I could leave them alone together. I mean, she comes over as trustworthy, but she doesn't have the sort of reputation that would encourage you to leave her in charge of a young child. That didn't matter a lot. She did so much work with the dogs, all the cleaning out and grooming, and helped with the puppy feeds and preparing the main meal, that I had more time to spare for being a mother.'

'I'm glad,' I told her.

'She was very good with the puppies. She took time with each one to put down its dish and make it wait for the word before eating.'

'Thank God for that!' I said. Every pup was destined to become a member of a pack consisting mostly of humans and each had to learn that they would never be the pack leader. In a real dog pack, they would not be allowed to eat until the leader permitted; but the necessary lesson is very demanding in human time and patience.

The feeding of the dogs was already well under way. I sent Henry to relax in the sitting room while I attended to my four charges. I paused at Clarence's kennel and received an enthusiastic greeting. Evidently his tail was on the mend, and a day in secure accommodation and the company of other dogs had done wonders for his morale.

I prepared to help with the other chores, only to be sent by Beth to join Henry while she resumed what she regarded as her proper duties. I washed, changed my boots, brushed my hair and did as I was told. I found that there was a bright log fire burning and Henry was stretched out, his body in one of the wing-chairs and his long legs spanning half the room. I sat down opposite and leaned back. Henry was snoring. I was wondering how Isobel ever managed to sleep through such a din, when a day in the concentrated fresh air overcame me and I also slipped into sleep. I had never previously been a daytime sleeper, but since my illness, and with Henry's example to follow, I was liable to doze off at any moment of relaxation.

The same fresh air had only made Beth rosy. Despite the hard work and the occupational hazards, she smelled sweet when she woke me half an hour later with a mug of soup. Henry I noticed, was already sitting up with a whisky in his hand.

'We've all had broth as a restorative and warmer-upper,' Beth said. 'I kept yours for you. The work's finished except for the pups' last feed, and that's already made up. Dinner's on and I'll take a sherry. Isobel's just coming.'

'Isobel's here and could murder a g-and-t,' said Isobel. Her round face in its unsuitable spectacles came round the door. 'How did you get on? Was Henry useful?'

I was only coming to slowly. As if in answer to his

wife's question, Henry made himself very useful, dispensing drinks and giving an account of our day. By the time I had my wits about me, I had enjoyed the soup and accepted a Guinness, and Hannah had joined us, looking prettier than ever in a dress which Beth had never liked. She asked for an orange squash and went to sit quietly, managing to appear slightly withdrawn from the circle.

'Did you find out anything useful?' Beth asked. 'Mr Cunningham is trying to find out what really happened to Clarence,' she explained.

I glanced quickly at Hannah to see if I could detect any expression, but she looked no more than mildly interested.

I let Henry give what was almost a word-by-word account of our enquiries, and I added what I had learned from Mrs Bell in his absence.

'You've collected a ragbag of information about people,' Beth said, 'but I don't see that it takes you much nearer to getting rid of what's worrying you.'

'It doesn't,' I said. My voice was still thick from sleep so I took a pull at my stout. 'I'd be satisfied if I could assure myself that we don't have another nutter on our hands. From what we know so far, there aren't even any likely cranks in the neighbourhood, unless you count Mr and Mrs Bassett, who seem to have been at their health-food shop that day, so what happened was probably a one-off. What bothers me is the recent spate of attacks on horses. The original horse-slasher set off several copycats. Clarence hasn't got into the papers, not yet, but enough people must know about the incident and, of course, if the SSPCA take Charlie to court . . .'

I had forgotten about Hannah. She sat forward suddenly. 'They won't do anything to Dad,' she said firmly.

'Of course, we hope not—' Beth began.

'They wouldn't. I wouldn't let them.'

I tried very hard not to sound patronizing. 'There might not be an awful lot that you could do about it.'

'I could tell them that I did it. They'd believe that. It's what most of them are thinking already, just because I get fed up at having people walk all over me. I know that you don't think anything of the sort or you wouldn't leave me alone with your dogs all the time.'

'That's right,' I said. 'But, Hannah, you'll only make things worse if you confess to something you haven't done.'

'Dad said that we'll have to be careful or they might take Clarence away from us.'

There was a moment of worried silence. Had Charlie been warning his daughter not to damage any more dogs? It was impossible not to wonder.

Isobel looked at me. 'Talking about being careful, you'll have to watch what you say. You can't ask too many questions without spreading the news,' she said, 'which is exactly what you don't want.'

I glanced at the clock. Evidently Henry and Isobel would be staying for a meal or Isobel would by now have left to begin preparations for their own dinner. 'We'll have to tread warily,' I said. 'All of us. But I'm not going to stop asking questions.'

'There's one thing you should know,' Beth said. 'This afternoon, between other things, Hannah and I took Clarence for a short walk on the lead. He's a very clean dog and he doesn't like to do it in his run. The butcher's van was early and I was running a bit late.'

'Not the same van that goes to Foleyburn?' Isobel said.

'No. I've seen the other one when I've gone over to help you on the shoot. But it's the same firm, same livery and make. I stopped the van outside the gates, which is what I like to do, because if he comes up the drive the smell of all that fresh meat sends some of the dogs wild. The point is that I couldn't get Clarence within yards and yards of the van. I had to leave him with Hannah while I went to buy meat.'

Henry sat up suddenly. 'And according to Mrs Bell, nobody heard the butcher's van arrive because O'Toole was running his circular saw. So the butcher opened up ready for business which was slow coming. He had his knives and cleaver handy. If a spaniel made a determined attempt to carry off a choice cut, he might make a sudden swipe with the first thing to hand.'

'But that's Mr McCulloch,' Hannah said. 'He wouldn't have done that. He acts very grumpy but he's really very kind. He gives me bones for Clarence.'

'He gives them to you, not to Clarence,' Beth pointed out.

'I don't see the difference,' Hannah said stubbornly.

'If I can intercept him on Friday I'll buy a couple of chops off him and see what I make of him,' I said. 'But I don't think we need read too much into Clarence's re-action. I've known more than one dog that made a wide detour around butchers' vans. The reason is simple. Butchers' van-drivers get so fed up with dogs coming round trying to steal meat that they get to be quite free with a kick or a stick. The motto is "Put the boot in first and if an angry owner turns up apologize later".'

'From which,' said Henry, 'it would be only a small step to "Swipe with whatever's handy and hide the evidence afterwards". As you say, we'd better meet up with the man. If we took a dog along, we might get a clue as to how he reacts.'

Beth looked aghast at the idea of one of the dogs being put at the mercy of an infuriated butcher. 'We'd be very circumspect,' I said quickly. 'Clarence seems to have got over the worst of the shock. Perhaps we could start taking him around with us to see how he reacts to people and places.'

'You'll keep him in the Land Rover if he's too nervous?' Beth asked.

'Yes, of course.'

'You promise?' Hannah said.

'Cross my heart. Henry, you said "we". Are you coming with me again?'

'Whenever you wish,' Henry said.

'Glad to have you aboard,' I replied.

'Haven't we gone polite all of a sudden!' Isobel said. 'I could use another drink but I suppose I'll have to wait until I'm asked.'

.

FIVE

Henry, who loved a mystery and was always grateful for any break in the monotony of retirement, had no intention of being left behind. He rolled up in the morning before I had finished my early breakfast. He even helped me to help Beth and Hannah get through the early chores. Hannah had settled into the kennels' routine as though she had been born to it, and the dogs seemed to welcome her. Scoter, a retired brood bitch awaiting a good shooting home for her twilight years, accepted from her fingers and even swallowed the pills which she usually tried to hide in her cheek until our backs were turned.

By ten o'clock we were on the road. Clarence, looking no more than interested and alert, was in the back of the Land Rover, together with the two cocker spaniels that I would be running in the puppy stake. The brief spell of fine weather had lost itself in a night which had produced a deep frost. Humid air was now creeping up from the sea, making fog wherever it met the cold of the land and laying down a sparkling carpet of frost which was instantly turned back into dampness on the roadway by the warm tyres.

The wipers could clear the windscreen but they could not clear the fog. The headlamps only threw up the whiteness. 'Not the ideal day for driving a Land Rover,' I said to Henry.

'Or anything else except a submarine or a train on the London Underground, I should think.'

We groped our way across the bridge. As we turned

away from the sea and then away from the estuary, the mist thinned. We ran through the village in no more than a haze of damp.

I stopped at the shed to take feed on board. One of the nearby farmers had left a sack by the door. We had a standing arrangement that any spoiled potatoes, tail corn or waste foodstuff of any kind would be left there for the ducks, to be paid for eventually in kind. We heaved it aboard.

'Ducks first?' Henry said.

I agreed, and not just because of the extra sack of feed. If somebody was poaching rabbits, he might not expect us so early on such a day. By going clockwise when we usually travelled withershins, and with the mist to damp down sight and sound, we might cut off his retreat. We might not grudge him a rabbit or two, provided that he was leaving the ducks and pheasants alone, but there was always the risk of the odd bird injuring itself in one of his snares. Anyway, it would be interesting to get a look at him, if only because he might have seen, or even committed, the assault on Clarence.

A dozen duck lifted off the dam as we arrived. They circled once, but as we started to put out the food they swung away and vanished. They would be back at dusk, bringing their friends. Duck feed at night, most of them flying to a different roost by day.

We set out again without wasting time. As I pointed out to Henry, if the poacher was out and about he would probably know by now that we were on the way. The hill was very steep at this end, which was the reason why Angus usually circled anticlockwise and descended where we were trying to climb. I put the Land Rover at the slope and we bounced and skidded on the wet grass. A Land Rover on dumper-truck tyres will go anywhere, but this was Angus's road transport and even in four-wheel drive his radials spun and slithered.

Halfway up, Henry suddenly said, 'I can see somebody. He's going down behind the hedge on our right.'

I chose my place and span the wheel, keeping the vehicle moving so that centrifugal force would help to keep us upright. For a moment, I thought that we were going to roll; but we came round, and an instant later I had lifted my foot and was fighting to slow down where before I had fought to keep going.

'You must have been murder in a tank,' Henry said in a hollow voice.

'I was Poor Bloody Infantry,' I told him. 'They didn't give us tanks. Hold on to your hat.'

'They knew what they were doing,' Henry said.

The hill levelled out for a few yards at the bottom. I slammed on the brakes as an alternative to ploughing into another hedge. The Land Rover slewed round and stopped, its square bonnet pointing back up the hill and its squarer tailgate almost in the hedge. Henry's lips were moving.

'Never mind that just now,' I said. 'The time for prayers is past. Where is he?'

'Near the junction of the hedges,' Henry said. 'I think he's sitting tight. He knows he can't outrun us.'

I didn't know any such thing. I wasn't at all sure that I could force the Land Rover up the hill again now that the treads of its tyres were filled with wet dung, but if our quarry was prepared to abandon hope I was not going to complain. 'Move into the driver's seat,' I said.

'I wouldn't even try to get this thing up the hill if you paid me.'

'He doesn't know that. So let him think that we can chase him up if he moves. If I get hold of him, hop out and bring Clarence to join us.'

'Got you,' Henry said.

There was a gate a few yards away in the wrong direction. Rather than try to force my way through hedges which had been allowed to thicken at the base for the sake of the wildlife, I headed that way, climbed the gate which had been wired shut and turned back towards another gate some fifty yards away. This one was standing open, and on the other side, squatting in the junction of the two hedges, was a gangling man in his thirties. He had floppy brown hair and spaniel's eyes. He looked so gentle that it was difficult to imagine him breaking a rabbit's neck let alone paunching it, but his hands were red-stained. His face was familiar from his days with the beaters.

'Strichen?' I said, guessing.

'Strachan,' he admitted gloomily.

'Strachan, then. Does the oil industry pay so badly that you have to come poaching?'

He flushed. I thought that he was going to deny the charge although the haversack over his shoulder looked heavy and had been stained with blood. In the end, he decided in favour of frankness and began to unbuckle the straps of his haversack. 'It's only for a bit of fun,' he said. 'The Broras enjoy a rabbit pie, so I try to snare a few for them whenever I'm at home. Maggie O'Toole's grateful for one for the dog now and again, and our cat won't eat anything else. Usually I stick to the rough ground at the back of the cottages – you know where I mean? – but I seem to have cleared that bit for the moment.' He held open the bag, exhibiting some fur but definitely no feathers.

'Do the pheasants never get caught up in your snares?'

'It hasn't happened yet.'

'And you visit the snares every day without fail?'

'When I'm here. If I'm going offshore, I lift them.' There was a pause. He looked ready to weep. 'What are you going to do?'

It dawned on me for the first time that he was expecting me to call the police and hand him over as a poacher caught literally red-handed. Depending on the vintage of whatever he had been reading on the subject, he might even be expecting to be transported. And I decided that I might as well capitalize on his naïvety. 'That depends on how helpful you can be,' I said sternly. 'Were you on the hill on the morning of Friday, a week past? The very wet day?'

'Yes. I did the rounds, though, and got home before the rain broke.'

'Did you see a springer spaniel wandering around loose?'

He began to shake his head. 'No dogs at all.' Then his gentle eyes suddenly popped wide open. 'You surely don't think I had anything to do with Mr Hopewell's dog having his tail cut off?'

'How did you know that Clarence had been docked?' I nearly added, 'Only the guilty party knew that', but it would not have been true. I decided that I must have been watching too much television.

'Bob Roberts told me.'

I nodded. It seemed possible. I could check. 'Clarence chased your cat,' I said.

He flared up immediately. 'Who told you that? Bob Roberts, I'll bet. Clarence tried it on once, but he got more than he bargained for. For Christ's sake, that cat can put the fear of God into bull terriers. I've seen him chase a German shepherd yelping across the fields. And if Bob Roberts is spreading tales, here's one for the book. He qualifies as president of the anti-Clarence club. He spotted him in the distance once, while we were beating, and I could literally hear him grinding his teeth.'

'What brought that on?' I asked. 'How did Clarence come to rattle Roberts's cage?'

Strachan realized for the first time that the wet ground was soaking his jeans. He stood up and pulled his trousers away from his thin bottom. 'Bob used to have a red setter bitch. He adored her, and I couldn't blame him, the dog had charisma. But she came into season and the Robertses were a bit careless. Their measures were good enough to keep their bitch in but they weren't one-tenth enough to keep Clarence out, you know what I mean?'

'I've heard,' I said. 'So he put the setter bitch in the family way?'

'Yes. That might have been forgiven. But the bitch took mastitis, which turned into blood poisoning, and no antibiotic would do the trick. She died. It was the purest bad luck, but Clarence had to take the blame. Bob never got over it. That collie was bought to take her place, but it was a forlorn hope. You won't let on to Bob that I told you that?' he added anxiously.

'I don't suppose so.'

'What are you going to do about the rabbits?'

'Personally, nothing. As long as you leave the game-birds alone I'm not too bothered. But I'm going to tell Angus.'

He looked dismayed. 'Must you? Do you think he'll drop me from the beating team? Can't you put in a word for me? I enjoy my days out.'

'He's more likely to let you go on trapping, on condition that you visit his fox-snares as well,' I said.

'I wouldn't mind that,' he said earnestly.

I was pleased. A benevolent poacher is the best game-keeper. 'You know where they are?'

'I think I've got most of them spotted,' he said.

At that point, Henry arrived. The wired gate had delayed him. Clarence welcomed Mr Strachan as an old friend, thereby exonerating him from any suspicion of illicit tail-docking.

I had had enough of skidding around on the steepest slope at the western end of the shoot. I knew from my army days that many a roll-over started with a backward slither. We went the long way round.

This time there were no signs of fox. The feeders were soon topped up and I could concentrate on the cockers. The cocker, a small spaniel, tends to be headstrong. Rather than let any misbehaviour occur, I preferred to let Henry shoot for me so that I could concentrate on the handling of the dogs, ready to nip any unsteadiness in the bud. We were able to adjourn for a late pub lunch in the comfortable knowledge that the birds were fed and the law satisfied and that the dogs had had a useful bout of training. Whether they would remember it was something else again, but a trainer can only live in hope.

'We could have got home in time for lunch,' Henry pointed out.

'Would you have preferred that?' I asked him.

He grinned at me. 'Not by a mile! School's out!' Henry raised his pint and glanced around the bar. Mrs Bell, unfortunately, was not present. I had thought of a whole host more questions to ask her. 'What's for the afternoon?'

He had to wait while I chewed and swallowed a mouthful of steak pie. 'It's too easy to assume that Clarence went in the direction of the cottages,' I said at last. 'But maybe he didn't. Nobody seems to have seen him there. He may have headed more towards the other road, the one we've just used. There's a house there with outbuildings. It's set back among trees and you hardly see it from the road, but there's a signboard. I took a look as we passed and it says something about bodywork. I'd like to call in, perhaps ask him about some repairs to the rusty bits on my car, and see whether Clarence reacts to the place. After that, we might work the dogs for a few more minutes, to ram home this morning's lessons, before we head for home and a hot bath.'

'I can live with that,' Henry said. 'Do I have time for another pint?' Considering his age, the strength of his bladder was amazing.

I glanced at my watch. 'You may as well,' I said, 'but I won't join you. And don't take too long. I'm assuming that the bodyworker reopens for business at two, if not earlier.'

It was a few minutes after two when I slowed to turn off the road. 'Let me get him talking,' I said. 'Then take Clarence out on the lead and see if he reacts. OK?'

'I think that that's within my capabilities,' Henry said.

The house turned out to be modest but well-maintained, backed by substantial outbuildings which had begun life as stone farm buildings but had been re-roofed and converted to light industrial use. On a chain in a corner of the yard, hating me with her eyes, was an enor-

98

mous German shepherd, obviously a guard dog and, from the row of teats, equally obviously a bitch. She rumbled at me without bothering to move, as though she knew exactly the length of her chain and was perfectly confident of her ability to have my leg off if I approached within range.

Other noises led me to a pair of large doors with an inset wicket standing open. Inside, a stockily built man in overalls was spraying blue cellulose onto a Jaguar which was heavily masked. He seemed to be making a good job of it. Beyond, a Porsche stood with one wing removed. The firm, it seemed, attracted a good class of business.

After a few seconds, the change of light seemed to register with him. He glanced in my direction but went on with his work. I retreated into the open air. He joined me a minute or two later, lighting a cigarette. He had pushed his goggles up onto his forehead. His face, now that I could see it, was round and mild.

'Yes?' he said.

'Mr Yates?' That had been the name on the signboard.

'That's me all right.'

'If I brought in a rusty estate car, for you to price repairs and a respray, when would you have time to take on the work?'

He thought about it. 'Early in the New Year. But, like you said, you'd better let me have a look at it in case it's too far gone. How bad is it?'

'Not good. I'll bring it in,' I said.

'Don't wait too long or I may be too busy to touch it. I get a lot of work in when the roads are icy. I count on it. I have to.'

There was nothing more to say. I found Henry sitting in the Land Rover. 'Surely I gave you enough time—?' I began.

'I tried,' Henry said quickly. 'God knows I tried. But Clarence wasn't coming out of the car for anybody. He was terrified.'

Mr Yates, now that his work had been interrupted, was

99

enjoying his cigarette outside the wicket. I opened the back of the Land Rover. Clarence, who was loose in the back, shrank into the far corner. I invited Mr Yates across and asked his opinion about Angus's tailgate latch, which was far from secure. Yates glanced at Clarence and at the cockers in their travelling box without interest and suggested that the local garage could do a cheaper job on the latch. Clarence studied him for a second or two and then came forward to proffer a pale shadow of his usual greeting. Mr Yates gave him a quick pat and turned away.

I thought it over while we gave the little dogs ten more minutes of practical work along the bottom of the valley. In the Land Rover on the way home I said, 'We shouldn't lend too much weight to Clarence's reaction. At the moment he's nervous about any people and places that he associates with his home territory. I think we can assume that Mr Yates didn't take his cutting disc to Clarence's tail. But did you see that guard dog?'

'The Alsatian? I did indeed. He ranked high on my list of Dogs To Be Avoided.'

'It wasn't a he, it was a she,' I said. 'Knowing Clarence's propensities, how does this grab you? Clarence sneaks off on the prowl, looking for food or nooky. That hairy monster is in season—'

'Is she?' Henry asked.

'I wasn't going close enough to look,' I admitted. 'Anyway, we're talking about nearly a fortnight ago. Let's suppose it. Clarence makes a beeline for the source of the irresistible aroma. He realizes his error and turns to flee, but too late; the bitch makes a grab and catches him by the tail, almost or completely severing it. Mr Yates rescues him, which is why Clarence took him for a friend. Yates completes the severing of the tail either because the partial severance is causing Clarence so much pain; or else he doesn't want Clarence to go home showing tooth-marks belonging to his beloved but dangerous guard dog—'

'Because,' Henry broke in triumphantly, 'the dog is on its last warning and after another complaint the sheriff would certainly order it to be destroyed. The courts are inclined to get hot under the collar about savage dogs at the moment. Yes, it's possible.'

'We seem to be finding too many faintly possible suspects,' I said. 'This may be the first one with any claim to probability.'

We were in time to help finish the day's work, which included preparing our day's harvest of rabbits for the freezer. After the usual communal refreshment, Isobel and Henry left for home and I had the promised hot bath.

Beth served up one of the superb game pies which tended to be a feature of our winters – with the game-dealer paying less than a pound per bird, it made sense to keep back as many as we could eat. Hannah, looking more nubile than ever in what I thought must be a new dress, had been shown how to prepare a game pie, and could hardly wait to demonstrate her new accomplishment to her father. I felt sorry for Charlie. I had no doubt that he would be hounded to produce a steady stream of pheasants so that she could show off her new-found skill. Nothing drains the element of enjoyment out of a sport like being forced to perform.

Warm and replete, I was dozing in front of the sitting-room fire when I heard the unmistakable rattles of my own car arriving at the front door. I stayed where I was. Angus was both able and permitted to make his own way inside. I heard him come into the hall and speak to Beth through the kitchen door.

'I'm in the sitting room,' I called.

Angus came in, pretending to glower. 'Who cares where you are?' he demanded. 'It's Beth I come to see.'

'It's the whisky you come to see,' I told him. 'Help yourself. Pour me a can of Guinness while you're at it. How's the wild-fowling going?'

Angus busied himself at the cabinet. 'No' bad,' he said

over his shoulder. 'I've put them under the geese a few times. They've got at least one apiece and they're fine pleased. But they're an elderly group.' Angus put a glass down beside me, yawned and took a chair. He closed his eyes for a moment and sighed with satisfaction. 'For the moment, they've taken a scunner to getting up and squishing over the mud before dawn. Truth to tell, so've I. Am I getting old?'

'Of course you are,' I said. 'I've been telling you so ever since we were in the Falklands.'

'Shame!' Beth said, closing the door behind her. 'Angus is ageless, like the best sort of antique.' She joined Angus on the couch.

'And just as full of worms. You only try to reassure him because he butters you up,' I told her.

'She says it because it's true,' said Angus. 'Not about the worms, I'm cured of that.'

'And,' said Beth, 'I don't see why I shouldn't have a drink, if you two are boozing again. I'll have a spritzer.'

'Help yourself,' I suggested.

'Oh no!' Beth said, dropping onto the couch. 'I'm everything else around here, allowing for a little pardonable exaggeration, but I draw the line at barmaid. I do not pour my own drinks.'

'And I'm a guest,' said Angus. 'Who did we say was getting old?' he added as I dragged myself tiredly to my feet.

In hurt silence I mixed the requisite white wine (from a cardboard container) with soda and gave the concoction to Beth. Somebody seemed to be missing. 'Where's Hannah?' I asked.

'She's bathing Sam and putting him to bed for me.'

I hid my surprise. Here was a change indeed! If Beth had come to trust Hannah with our first-born it would make life easier. I was prepared to trust Beth's judgement.

'What the clients fancy,' Angus said, 'is a nice, gentle day tomorrow, decoying the cushies. Friday they'll make the effort and come to the foreshore for the last time, Saturday it's our pheasants, and then they're away home to a life of ease. And what I'd like is for you to take them to the cushies while I go across and see how you've left a'thing at the shoot.'

'That's what you'd like, is it?' In point of fact, I would enjoy a day of rest from wrestling Angus's Land Rover up and down the hills and humping bags of feed with Henry; but catching Angus in a supplicant mood was too good a chance to miss.

'Och, come on,' Angus said. 'You know fine you're the one as has kept up wi' all the farmers around here.'

I made him beg a little more and then haggled over my share of the fee, but I yielded in the end and gave him an account of our activities.

'It's a pity yon bloody fox slipped out,' he said, 'but maybe it's given him a distaste for the place. Are you any nearer finding out who docked Clarence's tail?'

'A few possibilities. Too many, in fact. Did you know that Strachan, who beats for us sometimes, was snaring rabbits right under your nose.'

'Never!' Angus said, with so much emphasis that I thought he, like Roberts, had probably known it all along. 'What's that to do wi' Clarence?'

'Probably nothing. If you're going to let him get away with it, you might as well make him your occasional, unpaid underkeeper. He needs to be kept occupied when he's not offshore. He told me that Bob Roberts has a grudge against Clarence. Apparently Clarence insemi-nated Roberts's beloved setter, which took mastitis and died. Hardly Clarence's fault, you might think, but who knows which way a bereaved owner's mind will work. Don't let on to Roberts that we got it from Strachan, by the way. There's no point making bad blood between any more of our beating team.'

Angus nodded. 'Any others?' he asked.

'There's a couple named Bassett in the same group of cottages. I'm told that they're passionately anti-blood sports, but they spend their days in their health-food shop in Dundee.'

'When it's quiet in the shop,' Angus said, 'one or the

other of them will nip back home to put in time preparing some more of their herbal medicines. I've seen 'em. They walk on the farmland, whiles, complete wi' gloves and sticks, and if they cross wi' me they call me names. But that breaks no bones. They're piss and wind, the pair of them. Just as well, though, that Saturdays are their busy day in the shop. All the same, their cough remedy's no' half bad! Who else?'

'The hottest prospect seems to be a man named Yates, who runs a spraying and panel-beating business from a house on the Foleyknowe road. He has a German shepherd bitch that could take the tail off a dinosaur, let alone a spaniel, and Clarence flatly refused to get out of the car there. He may have tried it on once too often.'

Angus gave a quick yelp of laughter. 'You're barking up the wrong tree there,' he said. 'I found old Irma for Ewan Yates. Don't let him know that I told you, it's his one dark secret, but she's the softest old creature you'll ever meet. That's what Ewan wanted, a dog that looked and acted tough enough to keep away any villains but one that he and his missis – who's nervous of dogs – could handle. Anyway, she's hardly a tooth left in her head, poor old Irma. They feed her on bread and milk with a little beef gravy now and again. If Clarence went round annoying her, the most she could have given him would have been a nasty suck.'

I was loath to see a viable theory go down the tube. 'You're sure about that?' I asked.

'If you don't believe me, give her a good kick in the slats next time you're passing. Now, your car's outside. Do you want to swap back for the day? You'll need the Land Rover on Friday if you're doing the snares again.'

SIX

Over the phone, several of my farming contacts in Fife had assured me that their stubbles were 'blue with pigeon', but this assurance must always be taken with a whole barrowload of salt because the sight of a woodpigeon equates in a farmer's mind with whole swarms of locusts. Also, fields that may have held even a thousand pigeon one day may be picked clean and deserted the next.

I had appointed a rendezvous in mid-morning. The woodpigeon usually wakes at dawn and goes to feed, returning to some convenient roost to rest and digest its meal. This is the pigeon equivalent of breakfast in bed. So, unless one intends to rise before dawn and set out a decoy pattern on uncertain ground, there is little to be gained by starting early.

I used the time to make a quick tour, which told me that, out of all the fields that had been 'blue with pigeon', only one large pea stubble was continuing to draw the birds. From the standpoints of both sport and safety, this would be inadequate for the whole party which, when I arrived at the appointed pub car park, proved to comprise seven gentlemen and a lady, all of a certain age and showing signs of wear and tear after their ventures below the high-tide line with Angus. I set off again and they followed on in a Range Rover and an Isuzu Trooper.

En route between the one hopeful field and the rendezvous, I had spotted another large flock feeding on a rape stubble. I established one foursome in hides at the first location with a good supply of cartridges and a broad spread of decoys bobbing convincingly in a light breeze. Before we were out of earshot we could hear battle commence. Fingers crossed, I brought the others to where I had seen the big flock and, on the promise of a few pheasants and some help whenever rabbits or pigeon or foxes plagued him, the farmer made them cautiously welcome. A deep ditch formed ready-made hides for them.

One more quick trip to and fro satisfied me that the pigeon had not immediately removed themselves over the horizons and the customers were getting value for their money. I was free until mid-afternoon, when I would return with a young dog or two and help them to gather their bag, including those birds which managed to fly to some distant tree before falling to the ground, dead. Hunting out those distant fallers always impressed the customers and often resulted in the sale of a dog.

But before driving home and plunging into the work of the kennels, I decided on one more errand. I had passed a butcher's van or travelling shop belonging to Nairn and Sons, the firm that visited Foleyhill. This one would probably be the van which had called at Three Oaks the day before. I followed it up and found it parked in one of the smaller villages.

I joined a short queue of ladies and even allowed a late-coming housewife to go ahead of me. This gave me time for a good look at the van's door. There were no stray dogs around to test my theory, but when my turn came I bought a pound of sausages off the harassed-looking driver and loitered until I could watch him slide shut the door. This was no lightweight and its sharp corner passed close by another. Slammed by an angry or hasty hand, the effect would resemble a horizontal guillotine.

I thought it over as I drove home. The scenario was rather more believable than some of the others with which I had been toying. I ran it through in sequence. The van-driver had pulled up and slid open the wide door ready for the customers who, because of the noise from

O'Toole's saw, had not heard him arrive. Clarence, sensing the trays of fresh meat, tried a quick raid in the hope of making off with a pound or two of prime steak. The driver would not even have to make a deliberate attack with the sharp instruments to hand. An attempt to slam the door behind the departing culprit, not intended to do more than exclude him while moving the best meat to a safer position, might very easily have severed an undocked tail, after which the driver, guiltily aware that his own carelessness had invited the raid and that he had damaged a possibly valuable dog, would have disposed of the evidence and said nothing. A splash or two of blood around a butcher's van might not invite comment.

I wondered whether Clarence's raid had been successful and, if so, whether he had dropped his booty. I had known dogs so gut-oriented that even the severing of a tail would not have loosened their grip on a chunk of meat, but if Clarence, in pain and shock, had dropped his prize, there might once have been a clue in the form of a choice cut of pork or lamb lying somewhere in the countryside. But, if so, the crows and foxes or domestic animals would have found it long since. It might be worth asking whether any of the cottagers' pets had gone off their food around that time. I would certainly have to catch Nairn and Sons' van-driver at Foleyburn next day.

I was still deep in thought when I arrived home, to be met with the news that Clarence had jerked his lead out of Hannah's hand and made a quick raid on the kitchen, making off with a parcel of meat which was only partly thawed. We barely had time to recapture him and for Isobel to determine that he seemed to have escaped without deep-freezing his intestines, when Angus showed up.

Angus was sleepy-eyed but triumphant. He hoisted the corpse of a huge dog fox from the back of the Land Rover and held it aloft, rather like an obstetrician with a freshly delivered baby.

"What do you think of that?"

I shrugged. I always regret the necessity for killing a

wild creature other than for food, but there is no way to train a fox to confine his depredations to the rabbit population and to leave lambs and game-birds alone. 'You've shown the farmers?' I asked.

Angus nodded, yawning. 'Duggie McKillop says he'll buy us both a dram. My own opinion is, don't hold your breath. Albert Dodd was pleased but he wasn't going to let it show. I've left the snares, but if there's no sign of another customer tomorrow, you may as well lift them. And for now, I'm awa' to my bed.'

After so much distraction it was small wonder that I quite forgot about the sausages, which had found their way under the driver's seat. They only came to our attention a fortnight later when their aroma rose high above those of dead pheasants, damp fur and dog fart.

A phone call to the ever helpful Mrs Bell confirmed that the butcher's van could be expected in her neighbourhood shortly after eleven o'clock. I could have intercepted it earlier in the village, but if my suspicions turned out to have any foundation in fact, I might need to ask the sort of questions which are better asked without an audience – or witnesses.

So I spent an hour filling the feeders along the valley bottoms. The work would have been quicker if I had had Henry's help, but Henry had come down with a slight cold, and at his age, as Isobel was quick to point out, colds are not to be trifled with, especially on a day which was windy, cold and damp.

It was possible – at least in the Land Rover which had again been substituted for my car – to get from the dam via Albert Dodd's farmyard to the road near the cottages. The old farmer waved at me as I went by. He may have been shaking his fist, or else he wanted me to stop for an argument, but I gave him a regal wave in reply and drove on, cheered by the thought of his fury and frustration. Angus, who disliked the old devil as much as I did, nevertheless had a remarkable knack for smoothing his

108

invariably ruffled plumage and could safely be left to cope.

I reached the end of the farm-road in time to see the butcher's van to my right, turning off into an opening between the trees on the other side of the road. This, I could assume, led to Nearn House, the abode of the strange Mr Ricketts. I decided to follow. I needed to make the man's acquaintance anyway.

The entry was narrow. The van must have found it a tight fit. Even the Land Rover resounded to the twigs scraping its sides as it passed under the tunnels of trees on either side of a humpbacked bridge.

The trees continued around the back of the house but the driveway emerged through an archway into an open space, part courtyard and part garden, framed by a stone-built two-storey house, a single-storey extension and on two sides high garden walls. The house, although not very large, had been built to a higher standard of detail than the usual small farmer's house and I thought that it might have been built to house a minor landowner or the manager of an estate.

The van was drawn up near the front door and the driver was sounding what was evidently not the first blast on his horn, but there was no sign of life from the house.

At the sound of the Land Rover, the driver got out of the van. I sat where I was. Clarence was loose on a dog bed in the back of the Land Rover and I reached back and hauled him onto my knee where he made strenuous efforts to lick my face. The driver came to my open window. He was a ferret-faced individual in a striped apron over a brown linen coat. The van, I noticed, was identical to the one that I had studied so closely the previous day.

'Doesn't seem to be in,' he said. He looked at Clarence without any sign of interest and Clarence, after one curious sniff in the direction of his apron, ignored him.

'People do go out,' I said, wondering whether it was still worth introducing the subject of dogs.

'But something's no' right,' he persisted. He pointed to a door of a singularly ugly plum colour which stood slightly open in the single-storey wing. 'It was just the same last week. He's aye been here before that. Yon door was just the same, I don't believe it's moved.'

'In more than a week?' This was beginning to sound ominous. 'What about the milkman?'

'No delivery. See, he buys UHT milk, gets it delivered once a month – I was here when it came, one time, but I've never been inside the place,' he explained hastily. 'And he's not a man as would leave the place unlocked. You ken what they say about him?' He looked at me anxiously, as though I might never have heard of sexual deviation.

'I think so.'

'Well, I don't know. He's aye been quite normal wi' me,' the van-driver said, as though any practising homosexual would be bound to make a beeline for his wizened charms. 'My guess is that he's feared some o' the locals may have it in for him. They do, sometimes, when they think a man's queer.'

'I mind once I couldn't get over the wee brig for the snow so I blew my horn and he came to meet me – in yellow wellies, believe it or no'. Point is, I saw him locking his door just for that wee minute. There's folks around here never locked a door in their lives. And another thing. There's nae reek at the lum.'

I thought that he was letting his imagination run away with him but I looked up. There was indeed no smoke at the chimneys. 'Doesn't he have central heating?'

'He has the electrics but he said to me once it was o'er dear to run so he kept log fires burning most of the day. I never saw the place, outside of summer, but that there was a whole cloud of wood-smoke abune it. I was just thinking that maybe I should ha'e a look, only I didn't want to take it on mysel'.' He looked at me hopefully, anxious for someone to share or even lift the responsibility off his narrow shoulders. 'The mannie may be lying there in a fit, or maybe he's been duffed up.'

'It's more likely that he's gone away for a few days and somebody's broken in,' I said, 'but we'll have a look. Both of us,' I added as he showed signs of wanting to get into his van and drive off. 'We can be witnesses for each other.'

'Well, a' right,' he said reluctantly. 'But I hae nae broo o' this.'

I had no great liking for it myself, but the butcher was right. If the man had been lying, unconscious or incapacitated, long enough for his log fires to burn out, I wouldn't give much for his chances, but we had a duty to go and see. 'Come on,' I said.

He came to heel reluctantly.

The half-open door showed no sign of violent entry, although the paint, which was new, seemed slightly marked. But an intruder might have entered at the other side of the house and left by what turned out to be the kitchen door. It opened the rest of the way when I pushed it and a wintry chill came to meet us. The fires had been out for more than an hour or two. The door opened onto a short passage. Another door let us into a large kitchen, old-fashioned in style but with a superficial gloss of modern décor and gadgets.

In the middle of the floor, a man's body sat in a Windsor chair. I was never in any doubt that it was a body. His head was down on his knees, and it had been partly severed from his shoulders, probably by a blow from the kitchen cleaver on the floor nearby. The huge wound gaped wide open, showing the severed ends of bone.

'Is this him?' I asked the butcher. 'Mr Ricketts?'

My companion seemed to be making a great effort to hold himself together. 'It's his colour hair,' he said faintly. 'Lift him so's I can see his face and I'll maybe tell you.'

I had no intention of touching the body or anything else, if I could help it. 'I'll call the police,' I said. 'You wait outside.'

There was no answer. The van-driver had vanished. I heard the sound of retching. I found that my stomach for

111

gruesome sights had deteriorated since my army days. I would dearly have loved to join the unhappy butcher.

There was a modern, cream telephone on one of the worktops. I walked carefully around the outermost of the blood splashes, took a pen from my pocket and flicked off the receiver. I knew better than to dial out immediately. It is by no means uncommon for a criminal to use the telephone before leaving the scene. But the Last Number Redial facility only fetched an answer from a large Dundee department store. I broke the connection and dialled with my pen.

During the few seconds that it took for the emergency switchboard to answer, I took in a little more of the scene. Dried blood splashes radiated around the kitchen floor from the position of the body.

The telephone suddenly asked me which service I required. I bent down and told it that I wanted the police.

Immediately in front of the body there was no blood; indeed the man might have been bending forward to study the pattern of the bright linoleum. But that clean patch was outlined in a partial and uneven rectangle of thicker bloodstain, long congealed.

Another voice came on the line and I began to report a violent death.

When I emerged into the cold fresh air a few minutes later, to my relief the van-driver was still hunched, white and shaking, over the flower-bed. He could so easily have panicked and driven off, leaving me to face the police alone. I knew from previous experiences that two independent witnesses corroborating each other face much less suspicion and harassment than a single finder of the corpse in question.

Since leaving the army I had lost the knack of patiently awaiting my turn for duty or a call to action. Instead, I had developed the habit of filling odd moments with useful tasks. This, I decided, might be a good time to give Clarence a walk among the trees. If the police should conclude from their searches that a dog had been present it would be no more than the truth. I opened the Land Rover and attached a lead to Clarence, but he sat tight, shaking with fear and making it clear that brute force would be needed to get him down to the ground.

This was strange, when I remembered that he had shown no fear of the van-driver. Of course, it might or might not be significant. A dog can be very perceptive of human fear and he might be reacting to our reaction. Or it might be a different driver, although from what he had said I was entitled to assume that he was the same man.

The van-driver seemed to be recovering. I closed the Land Rover and approached him. 'Is your name McCulloch?' I asked him.

'That's right.' He seemed uncertain whether to shake hands. I patted him on the shoulder and left him to his renewed heaving.

As one would expect, the first arrival was the dour local sergeant, who came in his panda car and seemed disappointed to have only two of us to order around.

He told us to wait in our respective vehicles. I could have got technical about it – unthinking officialdom takes me that way now that I am free of the army methodology – but in fact I was happy to comply. I had already made a necessary second phone call, while keeping my face turned to the kitchen wall. The second call had been to Beth at home, explaining to her that for reasons beyond my control I would be unable to complete my tasks. The pheasants would not starve if left for another day but both the law and common humanity required that the snares be lifted or at least visited. Would she, I asked, try to get hold of Angus, failing which phone Mr Strachan and ask him to lift the snares. I spelt out how many to look for. And no, I said, I had not suffered injury or a relapse, the car was undamaged and Clarence was fit and well. I was perfectly all right and would come home in due course under my own steam to tell her all about it.

Having made my arrangements, I was content to sit in Angus's Land Rover and try not to look at the hideous door while listening to the radio. The sergeant, after one look into the kitchen, paced importantly to and fro on the gravel. From his colour I guessed that he was hard put to it not to add his contribution to the flower-bed.

Over the next half-hour the team began to gather. The van-driver and I were told to move our vehicles out onto the road so that the gravel could be searched. Soon we were engulfed in a row of police vehicles, to the great interest and inconvenience of the few passers-by. I kept my mind off the grim realities and instead amused myself by trying to identify the new arrivals – the photographer, the police surgeon, the pathologist, the scene-of-crime officers, the detectives, the forensic scientists. A large caravan arrived and, after much argument, was parked in a field on the other side of the road. For this it was necessary to remove a section of fence and the general disturbance soon brought Dodd the Father down, fuming, on the local sergeant, who was fussing around as a general arranger and confusion spreader. The sergeant had the weight of the law behind him, but Albert had the advantages of bad temper and irrationality, so that the honours were fairly even. The caravan stayed where it was although I suspected that some rental, or at least a quid pro quo had been agreed. Detective Chief Inspector McStraun passed through my field of vision and I assumed that he was to be the senior officer in charge of the investigation.

Mr McCulloch, the van-driver, must have made a fuss about the needs of his customers and the perishable nature of his goods, because he was interviewed in the caravan and then allowed to depart. My time came a little later. An athletically built man with a friendly face but an unbending manner, who introduced himself as Detective Sergeant Waller, fetched me to the caravan where I found the Detective Chief Inspector waiting, complete with shorthand writer and both tape and video recorders. The intent that not one of my words should escape I found rather flattering.

'Detective Chief Inspector McStraun,' said the DS formally.

'I know,' I said. 'We've met.'

The DCI looked at me sharply. Since I had last seen him he had cultivated a military moustache which, taken with his very upright bearing, gave him an assured look at variance with a strong Dundee accent. He must have been trying to place my face among those on the criminal files because the connection evaded him. 'I know the face,' he said, 'but you'll have to remind me.'

When I reminded him of the cases in his area which had spilled over into Fife and merged together, he relaxed visibly. 'I remember you now,' he said. 'The spaniel man. You were helpful.'

'And my wife more so.'

Mr McStraun looked pained at being reminded that a member of the public, and female to boot, had shown the police where to look for the truth. 'Perhaps,' he said. 'We never did make an arrest. And now we find you on the scene of another sudden death – a murder, unless somebody can explain how a man could hit himself on the back of the neck with a cleaver, hard enough to half sever it.'

'You didn't find me on the scene,' I pointed out. 'I called you to it.'

'That's true,' he said. He looked at me solemnly for a few seconds before deciding to abandon that line. Briskly and efficiently he took me through my encounter with the van-driver and our discovery of the body.

'Apart from the body and all the blood, did you notice anything different about the room?' he asked me.

I hid my amusement at the ploy and pointed out that I had never been at the house before. 'But,' I said, 'I did notice from the shape of the bloodstains, as I'm sure you did, that a kitchen table seemed to have been removed after the killing.'

He nodded. 'We found it behind the house. An attempt had been made to burn it. Can you think of an explanation?'

'Beats me,' I said.

He nodded, as though to say that that was only to be

expected but that he knew better. 'Now,' he said, 'tell me how you came to be there at all.'

I could have pitched him a tale about wanting some meat from the butcher's van and it would have been impossible to disprove. But I decided that I had nothing to conceal. 'I've been carrying out an investigation of my own,' I said. 'I don't suppose that there's any connection—'

'Tell me anyway.'

'I was just going to,' I pointed out. Some may regard senior police officers as omnipotent and only one rung lower than God. They themselves usually pretend that the public should speak only when spoken to and should then confine themselves to answering questions. But as far as I am concerned the police are men with jobs to do, as much bound by the law and the rules of courtesy as anybody else. I waited until he made a face which expressed some sort of apology. 'You may have heard,' I said, 'that your neighbour's dog suffered a rather brutal tail-docking, two weeks ago today?'

He frowned, but he was becoming interested. 'I heard something. Spell it out for me.'

'Charlie Hopewell, who I think lives two doors from you, has a springer spaniel, name of Clarence, a confirmed wanderer and a bit of an escape artist. You know him?'

'Only too well.'

'Two weeks ago, on that very rainy day, Clarence took off and came home later with about half his tail lopped off. Charlie was very upset, not least because your local sergeant and the SSPCA man seem to have got together to suspect either him or his daughter of committing the act for obscure reasons of their own. As a result, no help was to be expected from either of those quarters. I was looking for an explanation, partly for Charlie's sake but also because, as a kennels owner, I always hear very loud warning bells when animals are gratuitously attacked.'

'It may not have been so gratuitous,' the DCI said gruffly. 'If I'm thinking of the right dog, he has a knack of making enemies.'

'Attacked without obvious reason, then,' I conceded. 'There are instances when some nutter takes a spite at some particular class of animal. Gundogs could be the particular target of some anti-field-sports fanatic, in which case, as a specialist breeder and trainer, my dogs could be at risk. So I've been looking around, more in the hope of putting my own mind at rest than anything else.'

'And how far have you got?'

'Not very far.'

He met my eye squarely. 'Mr Hopewell's daughter has come to the attention of the local sergeant before now.'

'True,' I said. 'But not relevant.'

'That's as may be. You can hardly be surprised if the sergeant is suspicious. Personally, I'm inclined to agree with you – she's a friend of my daughter so I'm not unacquainted with her. The sergeant wanted to charge her with aggravated assault, but it was held that she had been resisting an assault with excessive violence. My own view is that she has the devil of a temper which she may or may not grow out of. But I find it interesting that you avoided mention of her history.'

He had a point, although I was not going to admit it. 'Just as you avoided mentioning that you have a special dislike of Clarence,' I said, 'for digging up your roses. I hadn't got around to mentioning it because you keep interrupting me. What's your excuse?' (The Detective Sergeant looked shocked.) 'And this is wasting your time and mine. I fail to see any connection between an injured dog and a murdered man.'

'As a matter of fact,' he said, 'so do I. But one never knows what's relevant until later. One thing I do know is that one can never ask too many questions of the person who found the body. He is usually the only person who saw the scene totally undisturbed. And until the preliminary search is finished and I get the pathologist's guess at the time of death – and a guess is all that it usually is – I have to bide my time.'

With all the patience I could muster, I took the Detec-

117

tive Chief Inspector, his sergeant, the shorthand writer and the two recording machines through my investigations to date. The DCI listened with an air of faintly patronizing amusement. The two machines seemed to show more interest than the other two men.

When I had finished, the DCI said, 'This Mrs Bell could be a useful witness.'

'I expect so. She knows the local scene, she's observant and she dearly loves an audience. Can I go now? I'm overdue for some lunch.'

He nodded loftily, as though eating were a human weakness against which he had been inoculated on attaining his present rank. 'Your address is still Three Oaks Kennels?' he asked.

I nodded in turn, to show that I could be just as strong and silent as he could. 'I'd be grateful if you could avoid giving my name to the Press,' I said. 'I have a living to earn.'

The Sergeant escorted me outside. He was suddenly human. 'I have a springer,' he said. 'The vet can't find any sign of parasites but the poor beast scratches himself raw.'

'Seborrhoea?' I suggested.

'The vet says not. But he can't say what else it is. I've tried everything that he's recommended, without result. Is there anything I can do about it?'

I had met the problem once or twice in the past and, failing a precise diagnosis, had found it best to treat the symptoms. 'Try Head and Shoulders,' I said.

'The shampoo? You're joking!'

'I'm not, you know. Try it. It works for me.'

'I dare say. But does it really work on dogs?'

'I meant on my dogs,' I said shortly.

I stopped in the village and phoned home from the hotel. Beth answered. Angus, I learned, had left his visitors at their hotel to recuperate before their evening flight, and Beth had caught him at home. He had called down an unusual strain of pox on my private parts but would

118

already have done the rounds and returned.

'I'm coming home now,' I said. 'And I haven't had any lunch.'

'I'll fix you something. But what's going on?'

'Tell you when I see you. This phone's rather public.' Not only that, but I could tell from the puppy noises that Beth was outdoors and using the cordless phone, which, despite the assurances of the manufacturer, can sometimes be picked up by other, similar instruments. I suddenly wanted to be at home, where things were safe and familiar.

Waiting had swallowed much of the day and the sun was low as I hurried home. The haar was rolling in again. Angus should already be establishing his visitors somewhere among the reeds on the banks of the Tay. The fog would encourage the geese to fly low and might give the visitors the chance of one or two more in the bag before the end of their holiday, but it did not make driving easier. I was glad to turn in through my own gateway and park at my own front door.

Beth had hot soup waiting and was breaking eggs into a pan as I entered the kitchen. 'This is all you get or you'll spoil your dinner,' she said severely. 'Are you warm?'

'Perfectly,' I said.

'Good. Now, tell me what's going on.'

I was washing at the sink. 'Say please,' I told her over my shoulder.

'Say you're sorry, or these eggs go in with the puppies' mash.' I could tell that she was laughing.

I dried my hands and gave her a kiss. 'Three, two, one,' I counted, and as I said 'Sorry' she said 'Please'. It was an old ritual with variations.

'Where's Hannah?' I asked. The story I had to tell was too gruesome for a young girl.

'She's in her room, playing tapes of pop music to Sam.'

I gave her another quick kiss and sat down at the table. 'I walked into a murder,' I said. The soup was delicious. I had never been so hungry.

119

Beth gasped. 'I was wrong, I really do mean "Please". Who was it?' she asked me. 'Anyone I'd know?' She turned off the flame under the eggs but left them to fry on.

'I doubt it very much. I told you that I was going to have a word with the butcher's van-driver and with the peculiar man who lived near the cottages. Didn't I?'

'Yes.' Beth popped the two eggs into a bread roll and put it in front of me. 'I take it that it wasn't the van-driver who got himself killed.'

'You take it correctly. I saw the van heading for the other man's house, so I thought I'd . . . No,' I said. ' "Kill two birds with one stone" is a saying that's off my list for the moment. I thought I'd catch them together. So, like the lady in the song, I followed the van. The driver was getting worried because the outside kitchen door was standing open but the place seemed deserted. He said that it had been like that the week before. So, lending each other moral support, we went to look.'

'And found the body?'

I glanced at Beth. She looks so young that I sometimes forget that she is my wife and a mother, and when that happens I try to protect her as I would the teenager that she resembles. I reminded myself that Beth was quite capable of skinning a fox or cutting up a pig and had on occasions discussed the most grisly details of deaths and disasters without any tendency towards the vapours.

'There was a body, I presume of the occupant of the house, fully clothed and sitting in a chair in the middle of the kitchen floor. He'd been there for some time. Somebody had chopped him in the back of the neck with a meat cleaver.'

'Oho!' Beth said. 'Things look black for the van-driver. They always suspect the person who finds the body. Go on.'

I had taken the interruption as a chance to catch up with my eating. I chewed quickly. Beth gave me a paper towel to wipe egg yolk off my chin. 'I saw the body first,' I told her. 'And the cleaver was lying on the floor. There

120

was a beautiful set of kitchen knives on the wall with the end hook vacant. The cleaver seemed to complete the set. I'd take a bet that it belonged in the house.

'He seems to have been sitting in the chair when somebody took the cleaver and hit him on the back of the neck, cutting at least halfway through it. He flopped forward onto the table. There was a good deal of blood. The cleaver fell on the floor.'

Beth pushed a mug of tea in front of me. 'Go on,' she said.

'The next thing was that somebody pulled the table out from under him, so that his torso came down on his knees and his head dangled horridly with the wound gaping. That didn't happen immediately but some time later, because a leg of the table had dragged through the blood on the floor, which must have been at least half congealed by then. According to our old acquaintance, Detective Chief Inspector McStraun – you remember him?'

'Yes, of course.'

'He's the Senior Investigating Officer. According to him, the table was carried outside and an attempt made to burn it, although why anybody should do that beats me.'

'There could be dozens of reasons,' Beth said. 'Suppose, for instance, the murderer had been leaving a message or drawing a map or something, on the surface of the table. It's still there, under the blood. If, as you say, the blood was already congealing, he'd have had an awful job mopping it off just to get at the message and erase it, and probably he'd get a whole lot more blood on himself in the process after he'd already cleaned himself up.'

'Or herself,' I said. 'Not that it seems to have been a woman's crime, but I'm sure it runs against the Equal Opportunities Act to jump to the conclusion that any violent murder must have been committed by a man. You could be right, I suppose.'

Beth whisked my dishes into the sink and began preparations for the dogs' meal. 'Whether I'm right or not,'

121

she said, 'Henry's still off colour and Isobel went home early to look after him, Hannah and I have been left to cope. She's done enough for today. You can give me a hand.'

'Haven't I done enough for today too?' I asked, laughing.

'Probably. But Hannah's keeping Sam amused. Would you rather feed the dogs or cook dinner?'

'We'd all prefer that I feed the dogs. Will Henry be all right tomorrow?'

'He says yes, Isobel says no, take your pick. It doesn't seem to have been more than the twenty-four-hour bug that's going around.'

We left the subject of murder far behind us. The dogs' dinner and our own were of much greater importance.

SEVEN

Somebody had talked. No story was attributed to a police source, but a brief item appeared on that night's television news and by morning the papers had it – to my great annoyance, together with my name as one of the discoverers of the body. When Isobel arrived with a much recovered Henry, both were in a state of acute curiosity.

By then, the phone was alive with journalists wanting quotes, which they did not get. When Angus dropped off his wife, in a similar but suppressed state of curiosity, Beth and I were impatient to get away for what we hoped would be a day of comparative peace. We were, of course, deluding ourselves.

Hannah had pleaded to come with us. I thought that she might have enjoyed a day in the beating line, but without her father's agreement and steadying influence we decided not to take any chances. We told her that Clarence and the puppies needed her more and left her with Mrs Todd, warning the latter not to pump Hannah and to keep her safe from any prowling newshounds.

We should have realized that the visiting Guns, when they arrived at Foleyknowe, would be just as curious as anybody. So also were the beaters, and they were followed in quick succession by a variety of reporters from the various media. These, having been fobbed off for the moment by Detective Chief Inspector McStraun, had taken only minutes to track us down and were prepared to follow us around all day; and since one or two of them would clearly have settled, as an alternative, on their customary hobby-horse about Slaughter of Tame Grouse on the Moors and the Crack of High-powered Rifles, it seemed better to give one and all a single statement. This was on condition that the media thereafter left us alone for the day – an agreement which they honoured when I made it clear that we would not make a start to the shoot until they were all off the estate – and also on condition that nobody else mentioned the subject to me at least until shooting was over for the day.

Roberts and Strachan, each of whom had had some acquaintance with the dead man, were present among the beaters but kept low profiles. I had hardly begun my statement when Bob Roberts slipped away. I saw him intercept a middle-aged couple who were approaching the throng. When I looked again, the couple were walking away along the valley and Roberts was back among the beaters.

After that, we were free to get the show on the road, only slightly behind schedule. I had been able to observe the party's performance on the woodpigeon and had assessed them as above average – the lady in particular was a first-class shot – so we kept them back where the birds would be highest and fastest. By lunchtime, they seemed dazed but exultant.

As I neared the barn, the beaters were debouching from their trailer and I found myself walking with Bob Roberts and his collie. 'Who were those people you spoke to during the press conference?' I asked idly.

'Those were the Bassetts,' he said.

'They were going to make trouble? In front of the media?'

He shrugged. I felt a cold shiver at what might have been. Any anti-field-sports protest is meat and drink to the media. 'How did you manage to head them off?' I asked him. Again the shrug. 'I think I've a right to know,' I said, 'in case it happens again.'

We stopped at the corner of the barn. 'Between ourselves?' he asked.

'If it's nothing to do with murder,' I said. 'Or Clarence's tail.'

He nodded. I knew that we would both treat my words as a binding promise. 'You'd be bloody amazed what goes into some of their herbal medicines to make them so popular,' he said. 'What d'you call those very small doses, so small they can't possibly work but they do?'

'Homeopathic?' I suggested.

'If you say so. Very dilute, anyway, but very illegal.'

As soon as he said it, the memory of the Bassetts' garden surfaced and I could guess the rest. 'Marijuana?'

'And mescalin. You name it, they grow it.'

'Well done,' I said feebly. Had Clarence, I wondered, had a monkey on his back? Had he taken to visiting the Bassetts' garden to browse among the herbs, in search of a fix? If nothing else, it could explain his extroverted behaviour. The Bassetts might well have decided to administer a lasting deterrent.

Lunch was being enjoyed as usual in the barn amid happy chatter when the local sergeant appeared and beckoned to me. I got up off my straw bale and went out to meet him in no very good temper, because one of the visitors had been making serious enquiries about the price of a dog that I had been working that morning and, what was more, did not seem particularly startled when I quoted it.

'What is it?' I asked the sergeant.

'Mr McStraun would like to see you.'

'When?'

He looked amazed. 'Now, of course.'

'Tell him to get real. I shall be available, here, some time after three-thirty.'

His expression went from amazement to total disbelief. 'You can't seriously mean to send such a message to the Detective Chief Inspector.'

'I can and I do,' I said. 'I'm busy. He has his job to do and I have mine. The only way I would come just now would be under arrest. Do you want to try it?'

He sighed and became slightly more human. 'Chance would be a fine thing,' he said. 'What do you think I might charge you with?'

'Hampering the Police in the Execution of their Suspects?' I said. 'Suggest it to the Detective Chief Inspector, with my compliments. Have a drink and a sandwich before you go.'

He looked at me as though I had offered him the use of my sister and stalked back to his panda car.

Isobel, who had overheard, caught my eye. 'We're glad you're recovering,' she said, 'but you were a lot more lovable when you were ill.'

'That's better than never having been lovable at all,' I retorted. But I made a mental note to ask Beth whether she agreed with Isobel.

I returned to my customer and was relieved to find that he had not gone off the boil. Indeed, he was prepared to complete the deal on the spot. This was only sensible; he would be returning south in the morning and I have the strongest objection to selling a trained dog without giving the pair, dog and purchaser, a chance to learn to work together. So an immediate agreement was reached, highly satisfactory to all parties, by which I pocketed a substantial cheque, the buyer spent the afternoon picking-up with the spaniel alongside either me or Beth, so that he and his new shooting partner could learn each other's language and foibles, while Henry inherited his place among the Guns.

To my relief, man and dog struck up an immediate rapport. Perhaps I should be more commercially oriented, but selling a dog always seems to be rather like giving a daughter in marriage although on much more favourable terms. This marriage seemed to be made in heaven.

After the last drive, while Beth was filling out game-cards, Angus and I were pairing up the birds into braces for guests and beaters and Henry was dispensing liquid nourishment, we were again visited by the police, this time in the person of Detective Sergeant Waller.

'The Detective Chief Inspector would be obliged if you

126

would grant him the favour of another interview,' he said. 'At your earliest convenience, of course.' The DS was looking distinctly amused.

'I'll bet he didn't express himself in quite those terms,' I said.

He broke into a grin. 'Words to that effect,' he said.

'Make him say please,' Beth suggested.

'Pretty please,' said the DS before I could speak.

'Yes, of course,' I said. 'I'll come now.'

Beth slapped down the last card. 'One moment,' she said firmly. 'My husband is not a well man. I'm carrying his medication. I insist on accompanying him.' Each of those statements was true in itself but taken together they were acutely misleading. Beth's reason, as I knew perfectly well and the DS undoubtedly suspected, was sheer nosiness.

'I expect that will be all right,' the Detective Sergeant said weakly.

The discussion had taken place within earshot of Angus. 'Just a moment,' he said. 'My wife's minding your bairn.'

'She won't mind staying a little longer,' Beth said.

'I'll mind,' Angus retorted.

Beth looked round. Isobel was a few yards away, saying farewell to Juniper and her new owner. Beth grabbed her by the elbow. 'Isobel, will you go home and take over from Mrs Todd?'

'Of course I will,' Isobel said.

'And feed the dogs?'

'If that's what it takes.'

'And Sam,' Beth said, suddenly remembering.

'All right,' Isobel said patiently. 'Hannah can help me. Is it all right if she looks after Sam?'

'Perfectly,' Beth said. 'Stay to dinner.'

'Thank you.'

'There's a casserole already in the pressure cooker. The vegetables—'

'One snag,' I said, 'is that we all came over in the Land Rover.'

'Transport home will be provided,' said the Detective Sergeant.

'Not with that pompous ass—?'

'I will drive you home myself,' the Detective Sergeant said quickly, 'if you'll only come, now, pretty please.'

'In one minute,' I said. 'If I'm not driving again today, I don't see why I shouldn't have a proper snort of my own liquor for once. Pour me a decent dram, Henry. Of the good stuff, mind!'

The scene at Nearn House had changed again. There were no cars in the road now and the trees around the bridge had been cut back to allow for the passage of the caravan which was now parked in the walled garden.

The Detective Chief Inspector, however, had organized an office for himself in a small sitting room, leaving the other ranks to get by in the stark and crowded caravan into which the Sergeant took me first to sign the fair copy of my earlier statement. The sitting room, in contrast, was comfortable, well furnished and decorated in somewhat florid style, although I felt that the comparison with a Turkish brothel had been rather harsh. But I would have considered some of the quite innocuous pictures and ornaments to be pretty rather than beautiful so that it might have been a woman's room rather than a man's. I noticed that the shorthand writer had been dispensed with, but the tape recorder and video camera had been installed.

DCI McStraun looked at Beth in some surprise as the Sergeant ushered us in and indicated chairs, but then he seemed to recall that she had shown herself to be capable of discussing the details of sudden death without emotion or bias and he greeted her by name.

'You're welcome to be present, Mrs Cunningham,' he told her, 'but this is an interview with your husband and any other voices will confuse the taped record. Any points you want to make can wait until after the formal interview. Is that all right?'

Beth said that she quite understood.

'Very well.' In a flat voice, the Detective Chief Inspector told the two recording machines the date and time and listed those present, mentioning Beth 'as an observer only'.

'Mr Cunningham,' he said – I was pleased to note that he had remembered my dislike of being addressed as Captain – 'in the statement you gave yesterday you told us of the enquiries you had made in connection with the docking of the tail of a spaniel, one . . .' he looked down at his notes – unnecessarily, I was sure. 'One Clarence. The visit that you paid to this house, the home of the murdered man, was made in pursuance of those enquiries?'

'Correct,' I said.

'Had you any reason to believe that the injury to the spaniel had occurred here?'

'None at all,' I said. 'I already had several possible culprits in mind, but I was trying to visit places and meet people in the hope of stumbling across the true facts. I took Clarence with me, hoping that he might show some reaction to a place or a person. I also wanted to meet the butcher's van-driver and look at his van, because one of the most likely theories seemed to be that Clarence had tried to steal meat from the van and had had the sliding door slammed on his tail.'

'I see.' The Detective Chief Inspector held out his hand and DS Waller put a photograph into it. 'Would this be – er – what you were looking for?'

He gave me the photograph. It was sharp and in colour. The gruesome, muddy and bedraggled object portrayed had once been part of the proud tail of a liver and white spaniel. Beth leaned over and I tilted the photograph so that she could see it. 'Where did this turn up?' I asked.

'Please answer my question.'

In general I am a firm supporter of the police, but when, as is often the case, they assume powers that they do not really have, it does them good to be brought down to earth. 'When you have answered mine,' I said. 'I have a legitimate interest in the matter and I can't see that telling me where you found it would in any way hamper your enquiries.'

He came down off his lofty perch. 'Why do you want to know? What good would it do you?'

'Tell me and I'll explain.'

He pursed his mouth in momentary irritation. 'Oh, very well,' he said. 'As part of the routine search of the area, any recently dug patches in the garden were investigated. This was dug up in the vegetable garden behind the house.'

'Thank you,' I said. 'I have Clarence at my kennels at the moment. His owner had to go abroad. That horrid remnant looks remarkably like the missing piece of his tail, but it would be difficult for me to be sure. I had hoped that the place where it was found might tie into my own enquiries to provide some confirmation, but no such luck. I suggest that you collect a sample of his coat. Your forensic scientists should have no difficulty in being quite positive whether or not they match.'

'We'll do that,' he said. 'The owner would be Mr Charles Hopewell?'

'Who lives two doors from yourself. Yes.'

'What sort of person is Mr Hopewell?'

'You must have met him often,' I pointed out. 'You probably know him far better than I do.'

The Detective Chief Inspector again looked irritated, perhaps with good reason. Sometimes I can hear my own voice being provocative without being able to help myself. 'I am asking for your opinion,' he said, 'not my own.'

'Very well. Presumably you know his physical appearance. I would put him down as a mild man, polite and very well intentioned. Law abiding. Outgoing and friendly. A widower, perhaps rather lonely. Devoted to his daughter.'

'And to his dog?'

Beth was directing a warning look at me, but although I already felt a great unease I had no alternative but to tell the truth. 'He's well aware of Clarence's faults but, yes, I think you could call him a devoted owner.'

'If he should happen to find out who had cut off his dog's tail, what do you think would be his reaction?'

'He would kick up hell,' I said. 'He would run to the authorities—'

'Even if those authorities had made it clear that they suspected either him or his daughter of doing the deed?'

'Even so. Or he might have it out with the individual and the authorities. I don't think that he lacks moral courage. But he would stop short of violence, let alone killing.'

'He shoots and fishes?'

'Yes.'

'And that isn't killing?'

'It isn't killing a person,' I said. 'It's quite within the law and perfectly ethical, a leftover of man's traditional pursuit of meat. Not the same thing by a mile.'

Mr McStraun looked at me for several seconds but did not pursue the point. 'Sometimes, a row can get out of hand,' he said. 'You yourself, you must have a favourite dog. If you found out that a man had deliberately injured your dog and if the authorities offered you no recourse, what would you do?'

I hesitated before I answered. There had been one or two instances in which I had sailed rather close to the wind. 'I might tackle him,' I said. 'I would have to go carefully because of my health, but I might go so far as to lay hands on him in anger. But I wouldn't kill him. Nor would Charlie Hopewell.'

'But,' said the Detective Chief Inspector, 'you used to be a professional soldier. You have been trained in unarmed combat. You could be reasonably sure of handing out a beating without killing your opponent. Tell me, why did Mr Hopewell go abroad so suddenly?'

I felt the prickling of the skin which had always warned me of danger, but this was not an occasion for diving into cover. 'His son was holidaying in the French Alps and

131

phoned to say that he'd broken his leg, skiing. He had Mr Hopewell's car with him and the daughter-in-law doesn't drive. If he wanted the use of his own car, Charlie had no alternative but to fly out in order to drive them back.'

'Would the insurance not have covered the return of the car?'

'I believe there was something wrong with the insurance. So Charlie said.'

'Did you, or anybody that you know, witness this phone call?'

'I certainly didn't,' I said. 'Why would I? But I believe in it.'

'You may be right. But, to further my enquiries, Mr Hopewell will certainly have some questions to answer when, or if, he returns to this country.'

Beth, looking like a schoolgirl in class, raised her hand. The Detective Chief Inspector actually smiled. 'Yes, Mrs Cunningham?'

'I didn't mention this to my husband, but Charlie phoned last night after John had gone to bed. Just to ask after Clarence and to say that they were on the way back.'

'I see,' said Mr McStraun. 'Thank you very much.'

I was not going to leave without hitting back, on Charlie's behalf. 'To further *my* enquiries, Detective Chief Inspector,' I said, 'where were you when Clarence's tail was cut off?'

The look that he gave me was too cold to be a glare but it came very close. 'If we ever determine exactly when that happened,' he said, 'my sergeant may be able to tell you.'

DS Waller put us tenderly into the back of the smart police Range Rover in which we had arrived and set off to ferry us home. At first we were all three too deep in thought for conversation.

'Do you really think my chief would be guilty of illicit tail-lopping?' Sergeant Waller asked suddenly.

I had only suggested it out of mischief and to strike a

blow for Charlie, but I decided to keep the idea alive for a little longer. 'Give me your own opinion,' I said.

To my surprise he seemed to take me seriously. 'He would hardly bury the offcut at Nearn House,' he said at last.

'He might,' Beth said. 'If he was stuck with the tail of his neighbour's dog and no easy way to dispose of it, and then he took over the investigation into the murder—'

'I don't think he'd frame Charlie for murder just to get rid of the tail,' I said. 'It's not reasonable.'

'It's just as reasonable as suspecting Charlie of murder,' Beth said. 'Do you think he did it?'

'Are you asking me?' I said.

'Actually, I was asking Sergeant Waller.'

'Oh,' said the Sergeant. He offered no other comment for several miles. 'I'm not really supposed to discuss the case,' he said at last.

'With suspects?' Beth added.

The Sergeant laughed. 'With witnesses,' he amended. 'But I owe your husband something. I gave the old dog a shampoo when I got home last night,' he added, in my direction I thought, 'and he had the least restless night he's had in months. This morning he wasn't scratching hardly at all. So . . . you won't let on that I spilled any beans?'

We both promised.

'I don't think it's gone as far as a real suspicion,' the Sergeant said. 'He's waiting for hard evidence – other than the tail, of course. But the tail could have happened in the van door just as you said, and Mr Ricketts could have told the van-driver, "Least said, soonest mended. There's no point having a stishie over what was an accident. Just bury it in my back garden and let it remain a mystery." You follow me?'

'Yes, of course,' said Beth. I could have pointed out that Clarence had reacted to the place and not to Mr McCulloch, but I was fairly sure that she had only asked her original question to get the Sergeant talking. 'And Mr

Hopewell killed Mr Ricketts in an act of revenge? How would you suppose Mr Hopewell got the idea that Mr Ricketts had docked Clarence's tail?'

'Somebody – Mr Hopewell or his daughter or some neighbour – could have seen Clarence bolting from that direction. Miss Hopewell was out that morning, because she was seen to return home soaking wet just after the storm began. Mr McStraun will want to interview her.'

'Well, he can't,' Beth said, and there was a steely ring to her voice. 'Mr Hopewell left her in our care, sort of, and while he's away we're not allowing anything that he mightn't want, not if we have to get every lawyer in the country onto it.'

'I'll tell him,' the Sergeant promised.

'Be sure that you do,' Beth said. 'Have you any ideas about the identity of the mysterious lover?'

'Oh, come on,' said the Sergeant. 'You can't expect—'

'I wouldn't expect his name,' Beth said. 'Yes or no would do. It wouldn't exactly set the country ablaze.'

'True.' The Sergeant drove in silence for another minute but I knew that he would speak. Few men can help telling Beth whatever she wants to know. 'In point of fact,' he said at last, 'we've interviewed as many neighbours as we could get hold of but we haven't got anywhere yet. We don't even have any real evidence of homosexuality although the pathologist's final report should settle the matter one way or the other. There seem to have been two regular visitors. One man who walked out from the village, on a few occasions and usually after dark; and another who arrived most days, usually from the opposite direction, in a small and rather nondescript van. Nobody could offer us the least vestige of a description.'

'I was led to believe that the small van was delivering supplies,' I said.

'We've traced all his suppliers and none of their vans fits the description or came so often.'

'Perhaps the two of them met there and there was a flare-up of jealousy,' I suggested.

'We thought of that.'

'And perhaps they didn't,' said Beth. 'There are reasons for mysterious visits other than sexual liaisons, you know.' (I thought that the Sergeant looked at her sharply.) 'But assume that John's right. Perhaps they were one and the same person. I think that you should search the forestry tracks and any old quarries and sandpits. About five miles out, there's a very minor road that links the two roads that run out of the village going north. I think you should search around the whole triangle.'

'For what?' the Sergeant asked. His voice had risen in surprise.

'For the van, of course,' Beth said patiently.

'Well, it's certainly a thought,' said the Sergeant. He digested it in silence right across the Tay Bridge and most of the way to Three Oaks.

'How badly burned was the table?' Beth asked suddenly.

The Sergeant by now had lost his reserve. 'Only one end was much burned,' he said. 'I suppose that if their face or faces were known locally they couldn't stay on to keep the fire going, in case somebody came to see whether the smoke or firelight signified an accidental fire. Between damp rubbish on the bonfire and the dampening effect of the blood, it just plain went out.' He pulled up at our front door. The lights were blazing and I could see Isobel moving around in the kitchen. I began to remember that I was hungry.

Beth got out and thanked the Sergeant graciously. 'I think that you should also suggest that they wash the blood off the table-top,' she said.

'Why?'

'Just a wild thought. You'll know why if I'm right, and if I've guessed wrong I won't look quite such an ass.'

We took the Sergeant to the kennel where he could clip some hair from Clarence, who was as usual so delighted to be the focus of attention that he made the task difficult to the point of danger. We watched the Range Rover out of sight and then headed for the house.

'Did Charlie really phone last night?' I asked Beth.

'No, of course not,' she said. 'I just didn't want them to be too cocksure that Charlie had run away. Of course, if he really did do it, I'm going to be a dirty word with the police. But I don't think that he did.'

We went inside to face a thousand questions from Henry and Isobel. Hannah was feeding Sam. She smiled her sweet smile but otherwise gave Sam all her attention.

Three Sundays out of four were days of comparative rest; but it happened that on the next day fell what I had once called my Masterclass. I had outgrown that particular piece of vanity but the name had stuck. To it came a regular nucleus of dog-owners who enjoyed the ambience or the socializing which went along with the dog-work, plus an ever-changing minority learning to cope with a new pup or a new problem. As well as being a useful little earner, it brought us some commissions to retrain the failed attempts of amateurs, and in the fullness of time a surprising number of sales of puppies or trained dogs.

That morning there was a fuller than usual turn-out, for which naked curiosity was surely to blame. I could hardly complain – the increase would boost our profit from the attendance fees. Early telephone traffic, however, suggested that I, as one of the discoverers of the body, would again be plagued by reporters, who would expect to take up a lot of my time without paying a penny for it and then, instead of repaying favours with a little welcome publicity, would damn the whole practice of shooting with snide remarks, under the impression that they were currying favour with the largely indifferent public.

As the appointed hour approached, therefore, I reminded the arrivals that there was a danger of their dogs becoming accustomed to obeying commands only on the usual training grounds and ignoring them elsewhere. I loaded my car with dummies, dummy launchers and all the paraphernalia of training, including whistles and other goodies that might be sold along the way, told Beth to send any latecomers to Tentsmuir Forest and to refer reporters to Mr McCulloch, the butcher's van-driver, whose home address I had had the forethought to obtain while we waited for the police to arrive. I then led my convoy away.

Five miles of broad beach, deserted at that time of year, was more than enough for our needs. We managed to keep in the lee of the conifers, sheltered from a cutting wind, and a good time seemed to be had by the handlers and dogs alike. Most of them had even made some progress by lunchtime.

Half a dozen of the most regular attenders were in the habit of lunching together, and a custom had grown up of inviting me to join them. The invitation was again issued, but in other respects change was in the air; almost twice the usual number wanted to join in the lunch and it was agreed that, since we would already be in our cars, we might as well abandon the local inn and sample the fare elsewhere.

One man, a university lecturer who had been struggling to instil discipline into the biggest, friendliest, shaggiest and most unruly golden retriever I had ever encountered, was happy to restore himself in the general approval by using the mobile phone in his car. We fetched up in a modest hotel near Newport, with the small dining room to ourselves and promise of an adequate lunch. Under the Barbours and Goretexes the company proved to be quite respectably dressed.

I had no intention of giving an address on the subject of Bodies I Have Found; but when the waiter, who was also the proprietor, had withdrawn and my immediate neighbours began to ask questions, I could hardly snub them altogether. As soon as I opened my mouth a hush fell over the whole table, so I avoided any mention of such curious features as spaniels' tails and described the scene as blandly as I could manage. Perhaps my listeners were disappointed at the lack of gruesome detail but at least nobody's lunch was spoiled.

My thunder was immediately stolen by the university lecturer, a tall man with a straggly beard and intelligent eyes. Most of those present were driving and making do with a single beer or a share in a bottle of white wine which was serving half the table. The lecturer, who had a long drive before him, was drinking water and sparingly at that.

He put down his glass. 'I remember Jason Ricketts quite well,' he said. 'He used to be a university technician – not at my present fount of learning, I hasten to say. He had his degree in applied science but no ambition to teach. He was a clever devil, though, who could have made his mark as an industrial designer if he had been prepared to live through the lean, early years. He was quite capable of whipping up a device to answer in the short term almost any medical or scientific need, or to translate a theoretical into a practical gismo. And at least he could be trusted not to molest the female students. The men were quite capable of looking after themselves.'

'He didn't like girls?' asked a woman whose Clumber spaniel had tried to start a fight. She sounded incredulous, although anyone looking at her overblown femininity could well understand how a sensitive male might be turned off female lures. 'It didn't say any of this in the papers.'

'I couldn't swear to it, not being that way inclined myself, but there was something in his manner and there were rumours. I don't suppose the police could release any such details until the sheriff had confirmed his identity,' said the lecturer smugly. He knew just what sort of bombshell he was about to drop. 'Rehabilitation of Offenders Act and all that jazz. And the media haven't made the connection yet. But they will.'

'Done time as well, had he?' enquired the owner of a seriously overweight Labrador.

'Quite a lot of it,' said the lecturer. 'He started in a small way, using the university's computer and a telephone line

138

to plant a virus in the computer of an insurance company. As I recall, it was a near relative of the so-called "Italian" virus.'

'All the display goes trickling down to the bottom of the VDU,' said the man with the Labrador. 'That one?'

'That's it. Quite funny, really, as long as it's somebody else's program that's doing it. Then he wrote to the company, telling them where it was and how to eradicate it, but demanding a comparatively modest sum not to inject a much more virulent one. They paid up.'

'They would,' said somebody at the far end of the table.

The lecturer nodded. 'He repeated his *coup* several times in a small way, I'm told. Very little of this was ever made public, by the way, for fear of copycat crime. If he'd limited himself to modest returns he might have gone on for ever. Eventually, success went to his head and he made the usual mistake of trying for one big *coup* followed by a tactful retirement somewhere warm and sunny. He tried it on with the Inland Revenue, threatening to wipe clean the entire tax records for the year. The police were called in and they nailed him without much difficulty.

'Any sensible judge would have turned him loose and told him to get on with it. But no. To avoid publicity, he was allowed to plead guilty to some slightly reduced charges and he was tucked away for less than he might have been. If he was as I think he was, he probably quite enjoyed prison. He certainly showed no great reluctance to return there. I've seen his name in the papers from time to time, being brought before one court or another for various high-tech offences.'

'You don't sound surprised that he was murdered,' said a man who had brought a pair of promising young German shorthaired pointers to the class.

'Bound to happen,' said the lecturer. 'Bound to happen. I'm only surprised that he lasted as long as he did. Homosexual or not, a high-tech and oddly behaved criminal of dubious sexuality in rural Scotland would be like a fish in outer space. In the inner city he might thrive. In some universities that I can think of,' the lecturer added superciliously, 'he would hardly have been noticed.'

EIGHT

The murder at Foleyburn was still exciting the attention of the media next day, but the finding of the body was not even the day before yesterday's news any more and I was left in peace to resume my normal routine. The need for training on live game had been satisfied for the moment; it was more important for us to work several times through all the dogs in training, giving basic instruction in the garden or the barn to those that had not yet reached the stage for introduction to live quarry and putting the slightly more advanced dogs through their paces in the rabbit pen and with dummies on The Moss.

One compensation for the publicity was that the shooting public were reminded of our name. The phone was busy with enquiries and I sold one dog to a visiting client. I grumbled at having to make an extra trip to The Moss in order to get the purchaser properly tuned to his acquisition, but he had come a distance and was going home the same night.

I spent a little time with Hannah, who was doing the rounds of the younger puppies, playing with them and generally preparing them for the time when they would have to accept membership of a pack that composed mostly of humans.

'Are you happy here?' I asked her.

She gave me her smile. 'I love it,' she said. 'I wish I could make it my life. I wouldn't mind working hard.'

'Your dad would miss you.'

She considered, while nursing a sleepy pup on her

141

shoulder. 'He'd miss me,' she said at last, 'and I'd miss him, but he'd be glad too. He's done his best for me, but we don't like the same things. He'd have been happier if I'd been a boy, I think. He doesn't always know what to say to a girl and I don't know what to say to him. That's funny in a way, isn't it? I don't have any difficulty talking with you. I suppose Dad and I have years of habit between us.'

'Authority and resentment?'

'Exactly.' She gave a sigh. She was sitting twisted, showing a lot of leg and apparently quite unaware of her own femininity. 'Don't you think that dogs are much easier than people?'

'I'm sure of it,' I said.

'I think Dad might marry again if I wasn't always in the way.'

'Would you mind?'

'I think it would be very good for him,' she said. 'He'll be getting old one day.' She left it there, perhaps feeling unable to verbalize her anxieties, but I could follow her train of thought.

'Who do you think cut off Clarence's tail?' I asked her suddenly.

She looked down at the pup. 'How would I know? If I did . . . I could kill them! Poor Clarence!' The pup woke up and nibbled her ear. I could understand the impulse.

'Don't get cold,' I said gruffly, and went indoors. I wondered for a moment whether Hannah's words had been a subtle confession that she had in fact taken the cleaver to Mr Ricketts; but her emotion had been one of indignation rather than guilt.

I was glad to flop into my chair after the dogs were fed and rest my weary legs. Henry and Isobel had left early. Beth was always able to draw energy from some undiscoverable source and work on after everybody else had flagged. I was alone with Sam, who had fallen asleep in his playpen and whose snorts and gurgles were soporific.

Hannah had planted a thought in my mind. Half asleep,

142

I was wondering what I would do when I became too old for all the tramping around. Perhaps I should switch to retrievers. You can give a Labrador most of its basic training from your armchair and the rest without going more than five yards from the car; but a spaniel must be taught to hunt, with all the attendant pitfalls, and that means walking.

I must have passed over the boundary between wakefulness and sleep, because the arrival of a car at the door woke me to the realization that a good dog trailer, with compartments for up to eight or ten dogs, could save me a lot of time and energy. I remembered seeing an American design for an aluminium trailer in one of the magazines. Perhaps Ewan Yates could put the body on a trailer chassis for me.

The thought was so complete and satisfying that the arrival of a visitor only registered with me when the door-bell sounded. Beth put her head round the door. 'Who could that be?' she asked.

'Unless you go and answer it,' I said, 'we'll never know.'

'You could answer it,' she pointed out.

'Too tired. Ignore it. They'll probably go away.' I wanted to think more about my trailer.

Beth made a little sound of quite justified indignation and I heard her cross the hall. There were voices. Beth, removing her apron, returned with Sergeant Waller, offering him a chair before collecting Sam from his playpen and sitting herself down on the couch with him. The Sergeant was still in plain clothes and he had a document case clasped in his hand. Sleep receded and vanished. I sat up, rubbed my eyes and glanced at the clock. A remarkable amount of time seemed to have slipped away. Pleasant smells were emanating from the kitchen.

'I'm sure the Sergeant could do with a drink,' Beth said. 'Or, even if he couldn't, I could.'

We were now definitely back in my area of responsibility. Obediently, I got up and looked at the Sergeant. 'I think I'm here on duty,' he said.

I poured Beth a sherry and opened a can of Guinness

for myself before looking at the Sergeant again. 'You don't sound very sure,' I said.

'I'm not. Well, perhaps a small dram.'

A dram can vary in size, depending on whether you are using it in avoirdupois or as an apothecary's measure. 'We don't seem to keep small drams in this house,' I said. 'Henry Kitts doesn't approve of them.' I poured him something between a small and a large whisky and he seemed to be satisfied. I added a couple of logs to the fire and sat down again.

'Now,' I said. 'To what do we owe?'

'I've come to ask for help – and I don't mean in liquid form. When I ran you home the other evening, Mrs Cunningham made certain suggestions.' Beth chuckled suddenly. The Sergeant looked shocked. 'I'm referring, as I think you knew, to your suggestions concerning our investigation. They've got me into a bit of a pickle.'

'They weren't any good, then?' Beth asked.

'They were good. Much too good. Let me explain. I didn't want to invite a lot of scorn and derision. Also, I couldn't let on that they were your suggestions without admitting that I'd said much more to you both than I should. So I went by myself to search around the triangle of roads and I found tracks which led me to a small van, old but in sound condition. It was tucked away up a firebreak in the forestry, about three miles beyond Nearn House. So, of course, I rushed back to tell the glad tidings without considering for a moment any possible implications.

'The van turns out to have been stolen around a year ago and its plates had been altered. There was a remarkable absence of fingerprint and similar evidence and the layers of dead conifer needles don't hold tracks, so we don't have high hopes of learning too much from the van itself; but there were some faint smears of blood and, down on the floor below the driver's seat, we found one white hair which the lab thinks will match up with hairs from Clarence.'

Beth saw me twitch. 'Relax, John,' she said. 'It doesn't mean that Clarence was ever in the van. Somebody – perhaps whoever cut off his tail – could easily have carried a hair on his or her clothes into the van.'

'That's perfectly true,' said the Sergeant. 'The other thing is that they had been preserving what was left of the table-top because there were some significant smears in the thick clotting of dried blood on the surface. When I suggested that the blood be dissolved away, they photographed the smears for the record and then set about it. Mrs Cunningham, how on earth did you know what they were going to find?'

Beth seemed to be giving more attention to Sam than to the Sergeant. 'I'm not sure that I did know,' she said. 'What did they find?'

By way of an answer the Sergeant opened his document case, which seemed to contain mostly large prints of colour photographs. He fingered through them and withdrew two which he laid on the coffee table in front of Beth. I moved to a seat beside her on the couch so that we could study them together.

The first print showed the table-top much as it had been when recovered from the remains of the bonfire. Part of it was burned away and more was badly scorched but perhaps a third was relatively undamaged. Blood had spurted and dribbled onto the surface and had been allowed to clot and dry while it lay in several small but deep puddles and there were, as the Sergeant had said, traces and smears which had been made, I thought, before the blood had done more than begin to congeal.

The second photograph showed the table-top from the same angle, largely cleaned of blood although considerable staining was still evident. Where the deepest pool had been, there could now be seen a thin, rectangular card of grey plastic.

'You know what that is?' the Sergeant asked me.

We all enjoy pretending omniscience now and again. I succumbed to temptation. 'Judging from his previous record as a brilliant but unstable technician with a penchant for crime—' I began.

The Sergeant jumped in his chair as though he had sat on a wasp. 'How did you come to know about that?' he asked. 'Surely I'm not so far gone in indiscretion—?'

I explained about the chance that had brought the lecturer to my Masterclass. 'Knowing that,' I said, 'it isn't too difficult to guess what kind of card that might be.'

The Sergeant nodded. 'We'll be obliged if you don't pass that information on to the media just yet, although they'll suss him out sooner or later.' He looked from me to Beth and back again. 'Well,' he said at last, 'in for a penny, in for a pound. We've had some complaints about several banks from members of the public and one complaint from a bank itself. Money disappearing from accounts on what seem to be valid cash-card transactions which the account-holder swears were never made. That happens all the time, of course. Sometimes the customer is trying it on. And people can be careless, leaving the card lying around and writing down the PIN number in case they forget it. Then again, people can forget about a genuine withdrawal. Also, the machines aren't infallible, although bank staff would have to be burned at the stake before they'd admit any such thing. But in one instance the card-holder was on holiday in Cornwall at the time and used his card in Truro, in the presence of about six witnesses, on the same day as a withdrawal in Aberdeen.

'It was beginning to look as though somebody was beating the system. The fact that there had been comparatively few instances, and those not for very large amounts, suggested that those instances might merely be trial runs, intended only to confirm that whatever they were doing worked. Which could mean that they were biding their time.'

'Ready for one quick blitz and then vamoose?' I suggested, thinking of the lecturer's story.

'Exactly. With any repetitive crime, if they go on for too long we catch them. Fraud Squad say that the likeliest

MO would be to stockpile until they'd cracked the code for dozens of accounts and then clean them all out overnight. By the time the shouting started they'd be long gone.

'In a back room at Nearn House, we found a workshop. There was nothing directly connected with bank and credit-card frauds except some plastic material and magnetic strip, but it seems that his interests were catholic. We found listening devices, for example, and the makings of a gadget which seems to be aimed at being able to make calls from a public phone without payment. There are one or two other gadgets in an unfinished state and our technicians are having a great time trying to figure out what they were going to be if he'd finished them.

'Now that you've led us to the card, we can guess the rest. If you look closely at the shot of the table-top before it was cleaned, you can see a clear patch and four little rings among the bloodstains. We take it that those were made by the rubber feet on a machine for copying the magnetic information from a bank card onto another card. In point of fact, you can buy such a machine if you know where to go, but it would be in line with his character to whip one up for himself. Our guess is that whoever killed him took the machine, probably wrapped in a polythene bag, ready to cleanse later, and took as many cards as he could lay hands on, but that he drew the line at dredging through the blood and getting himself more bloodstained than he already was.'

The Sergeant or his superiors, I thought, might be jumping to conclusions. 'Isn't it possible that somebody came along, found him dead and pinched the makings of the forged cards?' I suggested.

'Just possible,' said the Sergeant. 'My problem is that I've appeared just a little too psychic. I didn't intend to steal credit that was due to Mrs Cunningham, but there was no way I could say that the suggestions were hers without admitting that I'd shot my mouth off. But when the suggestions paid off so handsomely, I was invited to go and see Detective Chief Inspector McStraun first thing tomorrow morning and explain myself. So I've come to you for the explanation.'

Sam was coming out of his sleep and making enquiring noises. Beth joggled him gently. 'There wasn't anything psychic about it,' she said softly. She seemed to be speaking to Sam. 'I didn't know anything about faking bank cards. It just seemed very odd to me that anyone should bother to try to burn the kitchen table when, from what John said, the marks on the top didn't seem to be as significant as all that. Of course, there might have been fingerprints that I didn't know about, but there would be easier and safer ways of dealing with fingerprints than trying to burn a whole table out of doors where the smoke or the firelight might attract witnesses.

'It just seemed to me that if there was something under the blood, there could be all sorts of reasons why he might prefer to burn the table. John said that the blood had begun to congeal before the table was moved, so that happened some time later. If he'd worn overalls or something during the murder and then got rid of them and cleaned himself up, whoever-it-was would then have to clean up a whole lot of blood to get at whatever was underneath, probably getting all bloodstained again, or else carry the table outside and burn it. In his position, if I was strong enough or had somebody to help me, I think I'd opt for burning.'

'It wasn't a very heavy table,' the Sergeant said.

Beth nodded. 'He just ought to have risked sticking around to make sure that it burned.'

'Fair enough,' said the Sergeant. 'I'm going to look a real wally, because I sort of hinted that I'd deduced that the card would be there and I'm going to have to show myself up as a bit of a chancer. Well, it's my own stupid fault and I dare say that I'll be able to live it down by the turn of the century. What about the van? Can you show me some way to redeem myself?'

'All I did,' Beth said, 'was to think how it would be. Do you see what I mean?'

148

'No,' said the Sergeant.

'Oh. Well, look at it this way. If I was going to have a liaison with somebody – which I'm not,' she added reassuringly in my direction, ' – somebody who lived not far from home and a bit back from the road, and if I didn't want everybody to know all about it, I certainly wouldn't walk to his house oftener than now and again, usually after dark. And just as certainly I wouldn't drive my own car to his house every day. What I'd do would be to buy an old car or van. Probably a van, because I wouldn't be so visible inside it. I'd buy it cheap or steal it and I'd tuck it away up some forestry track or in an abandoned barn. Then I could leave home in my own car, go to where I'd left the van and drive on from there in it, wearing a false beard and a big hat so that nobody seeing me whizz by would get a proper look at me. That way, both the visitors could be the same man, which is much simpler and somehow less immoral than imagining him having two different homosexual lovers.'

Beth spoke without embarrassment on her own part but she was beginning to embarrass me. 'Should you be saying these things into Sam's ear?' I asked her.

Beth smiled serenely. 'Bless him, he doesn't understand.'

'He understands more and more each day.'

'Well, I'm almost finished. I wouldn't want to be seen driving off in the same direction every day. I'd want to be able to drive off along either road and still come round to my hidey-hole. That's why I suggested that you should search around the whole triangle.'

The Sergeant knuckled his own forehead. 'Obvious,' he said.

Sam yawned and stretched and then began to whimper. 'You'll have to excuse me,' Beth said. 'This chap wants his feed and a dry nappy and, unlike the police, he isn't going to be fobbed off with glib explanations.' She got to her feet but stood looking down at the photographs on the table. 'May we keep those copies?'

'One moment.' After a hasty search the Sergeant made

one substitution. 'There! Those are duplicates. But unless you want my blood on your hands, don't let the DCI know that you've got them.'

'We promise,' Beth said. 'And, to complete the set, could we have a copy of the one he showed us of the tail? Pretty please, to quote from a policeman I know.'

'I suppose so.' The Sergeant, I was amused to note, was now completely under Beth's thumb. He searched again. 'Here's another duplicate. It shows the tail after a start had been made to cleaning it up.'

Still looking down, Beth said, 'I thought so.' She seemed to have taken root.

'She's not going to make another leap into the unknown, is she?' the Sergeant asked me.

'Very probably,' I said. 'When she gets that fey look and dons her gypsy headdress, prepare to register amazement.'

Beth seemed to ignore our frivolity. She was absently joggling Sam and her attention was on the photograph, but I thought that she was secretly flattered. 'I was sure that there was something funny about the markings when we saw the earlier picture. But it was obscured by the blood and dirt. Now that you can see it properly . . .'

The Sergeant laughed. He put his finger on the photograph. 'Is that all?' he said. 'We did manage to notice that one for ourselves.' I saw that among the liver and white markings was a streak of a more purplish colour. 'The outside door that leads to the kitchen had just been freshly painted. Unfortunately we don't know exactly when the work was done. But we found corresponding marks in the paint and some white hairs adhering, so it can be taken as certain that Clarence brushed against it on his way in. He didn't have much of a tail to brush it with on his way out, poor devil! That, I suppose, is why his tail was cut off.' The Sergeant stopped, stretched and took a drink. 'What a relief! I couldn't have borne it if Mrs Cunningham had got there first again. We policemen do have our pride. It would have driven me mad.'

Beth looked at him rather oddly. 'Why would that paint

mark make somebody want to cut the tail off?' she asked.

'Because it proved that Clarence had visited the house.'

'But why would that matter?'

The Sergeant opened his mouth to speak. I was sure that he was about to suggest that Clarence's visit had to be kept secret because the cruel attack on his tail might bring down the wrath of both the SSPCA and a loving owner, but just in time he saw the fallacy and closed his mouth again. Clarence's tail could hardly have been cut off in order to conceal the place where his tail had been cut off . . . 'I just gather facts. It's not my job to explain them. We don't know all the ins and outs of it yet,' he said feebly.

'No, you don't, do you,' Beth said. 'John, you'd better tuck those photographs out of sight in case Hannah comes in here. Dinner in about twenty minutes.'

She carried the now squalling Sam out of the room.

The Sergeant seemed to relax. Apparently there was nothing threatening about me. 'Clever woman, your wife,' he said musingly.

'One tends to forget it,' I said. It was the truth. Beth looked so young and her manner was so modest that it was easy to think of her as the airhead which she certainly was not.

'Attractive, too. But I don't know that I'd want to have somebody so bright around me all the time.'

'You get used to it,' I told him. 'In fact, she doesn't usually let it show. Do you think you'll be able to explain yourself tomorrow to the satisfaction of Mr McStraun?'

The Sergeant turned a shrug into a stretch. 'Given a little luck and some quick thinking. But it's not easy to pull the wool over his eyes. He makes the same sort of half-intuitive leaps as your missis, with the same cat-like knack of landing right way up.'

While Beth was present, I had felt inhibited about discussing the late Mr Ricketts's possible homosexuality, although Beth herself would probably have joined in without a blush. 'What have you found out about him?' I asked.

151

The habit of indiscretion had become ingrained. The Sergeant spoke out quite frankly. 'He was healthy. From witness testimony and the evidence in the house, there's nothing to confirm or disprove whether he was in fact gay. When the pathologist's final report comes through we should know more. All he could tell us from a preliminary examination was that there was no sign of recent sexual contacts.'

'So the regular visitor can't have been a lover?'

'Who knows? Love and sex don't seem to be inseparable. There are traces of the presence of a woman. Of course, one dark, female head-hair might have been carried in on somebody's clothes just as a white dog-hair could have been carried into the van, but how it got onto the hairbrush that he kept in his hall is more difficult to explain. Along with minute traces of face powder under the hall mirror it's certainly suggestive.'

I thought back. It had been impossible for an army officer to remain unacquainted with some of the facts about homosexuality. 'Assuming that he wasn't bisexual,' I said, 'he may have been the passive partner?'

'You think that it might have been his own face powder? As far as I know, none was found.'

'It could have been taken away,' I said. 'And don't forget that human female hair is used in the better class of wigs.'

The Sergeant frowned. 'There's no sign that he was transvestite.'

'They can be very secretive about it, even when they're quite open about their sexuality. And very clever at hiding their alternative garb.'

'The house has been searched,' he said slowly. 'But you're right. We can do it again. And I'll ask whether the hair seems to be fresh.'

He seemed so relaxed and open that I decided to push a little further. 'Wouldn't you say that the signs are beginning to point away from Charlie Hopewell?' I asked. 'If he killed Mr Ricketts for chopping off Clarence's tail, which is unlikely enough to start with, he wouldn't have carried off the materials and the machine for forging bank cards.'

The Sergeant's face resumed its official mask. 'That's not for me to say. He might have decided to profit from an unforeseen opportunity. But we've agreed that somebody else could have come along and decided to help themselves to an easy source of revenue.' He got to his feet. 'It's time that I wasn't here. Thank you for the drink.'

When he had left, it took Beth only a minute or two to wrest from me every word that we had exchanged after she left the room. She seemed to find in them some significance that I had missed. I thought that she was probably bluffing, but the arrival of Hannah prevented any further discussion.

NINE

We were granted another day of comparative peace and quiet. I had convinced myself that the assault on Clarence and the murder of Jason Ricketts had been one-off events, possibly connected, and that no threat was posed either to my dogs or to the Hopewell family.

I was anxious to forget the whole business, but I noticed that Beth, who seldom sat down between dawn and the end of the working day, was spending time at the kitchen table, thumbing through the boxes in which our photographs were collected in the hope that some day one of us might get around to sorting them out and sticking the worth-while ones into an album. She seemed to have something on her mind. When I asked her what was wrong, she was evasive, but her face, usually carefree, was thoughtful.

On the Wednesday morning, Isobel and I were putting the younger dogs through the rabbit pen one at a time to teach them steadiness under temptation. Between training commissions for other owners and our own pups remaining unsold beyond our somewhat optimistic 'Sell-By Date', we sometimes had more dogs in training than could comfortably be managed, while still giving individual tuition, without resorting to production-line methods. So Hannah was fetching the dogs from their runs while Isobel and I took it in turn to walk them through the pen, sitting them on command or with a check-lead whenever a rabbit bolted. The latter event was becoming a rarity as the rabbits learned that on no account were they going to be chased. On the last point, they were deluding themselves.

I had a feeling that it would soon be necessary to eat the present incumbents and restock the rabbit pen from the wild with the aid of the local ferreter.

I had just come out of the pen and was lavishing praise on a pup who had got it right for the first time when Hannah returned, dogless but with a message from Beth. Mrs Bell had been on the telephone and would I call her back as a matter of urgency?

There were only two young dogs still awaiting their turns, so I left them to Isobel and hurried indoors. A phone number in Beth's neat writing was on the pad under the cordless phone in the hall.

The ringing tone only sounded twice before the phone was snatched up. Mrs Bell's voice gabbled a number and I gave my name.

'Oh, Mr Cunningham. I didn't know who to tell. I'm at Mildred's house. The police are next door, at Mr Hopewell's. I asked them what they were doing, but all that I could get out of them was sight of what seems to be a search warrant. They didn't break in or anything, I think they got the key from Mrs Haven. I didn't know what to do or who to call—'

'I'm coming over,' I broke in. 'But do you know who Charlie's solicitor is?'

'Hold on a moment.' There was a pause and muffled voices as though she had covered the mouthpiece. 'I asked Mildred. He bought the house through Gillies and Fairbrother in Dundee, just as she did. They handle most of the houses around here.'

I broke off the call. Luckily I had had dealings with Bill Fairbrother. He had bought a trained spaniel from us and later had pursued an unpaid debt through the Sheriff-Court on our behalf. I had his number handy and by shouting at his telephonist I got through to him. I compressed the subject into about fifteen words and he caught on immediately. 'I'll see you there,' he said.

I gave Isobel and Beth an even terser explanation, hurled myself into our car and drove off.

155

There was single-lane traffic on the bridge as so often before. Instead of taking my usual advantage of the reduced speeds to admire the spectacular view, I fumed and fretted my way across and down onto Riverside Drive. For the first time in years I wished that my poor old estate car was capable of more than a dignified if noisy sixty.

I drew up at last in front of Mrs Turner's house. There were two police cars in front of Charlie's house and I recognized Bill Fairbrother's sports car further along the street. The more brazen neighbours were finding excuses for lurking in their front gardens; others were watching from their windows. This was not net-curtain territory.

Bill himself was turning away from the front door as I cantered up the path. He shook his head at me before either of us had said a word. 'I'm sorry,' he said. 'I've done all I can, but they have a perfectly valid warrant.'

'Can't you find out what it's about?' I asked.

'You've as good a chance as I have, probably better. I have no real status. For all I know, he may have consulted some other solicitor since we last worked for him. I'm sorry, Cunningham, I really am, but I'm a broken reed.'

I know when somebody else is beaten. 'Too bad,' I said. 'How is . . .' After a moment I remembered his dog's name. ' . . . Gainly?'

Bill assured me that Gainly was doing very well, a prodigy among dogs, and went back to his TR7.

A stout constable stopped me at the front door by the simple expedient of filling the doorway with his bulk. 'Nobody is to be allowed in,' he said.

'Is DS Waller in there?' I asked.

'Who wants to know?'

I find that the best way to get answers to questions is to keep asking them, refusing to be diverted into answering questions myself. 'Is DS Waller in there?'

'Why do you want him?' It was a good sign that the constable had shifted ground slightly.

'Is DS Waller in there?'

The constable looked angry but also confused. 'Yes, he's in there,' he said curtly.

'Please tell him that John Cunningham is here and wants to speak to him.'

The constable, pleased to have a chance to resume his authority, smiled thinly and shook his head.

I raised my voice. 'Detective Sergeant Waller!' I was pleased to discover that my parade-ground voice, trained to get through to a company at a hundred yards, upwind and in a gale, had lost none of its quality. I could hear echoes coming back from the houses and then from the hills.

Very few seconds later, Sergeant Waller erupted from the front door, blinking. 'What the hell?' he demanded.

'You took the words out of my mouth. In Mr Hopewell's absence and on his behalf, I want to know what the hell's going on,' I said.

He shook his head at me almost as loftily as the constable had done. 'No way,' he said.

'All right. Is Detective Chief Inspector McStraun in there?'

'Detective Chief Inspectors don't search houses. They have minions like me for that.'

'While they lounge on silken couches, I suppose, eating grapes from the fingers of scantily clad WPCs?'

He refused to be diverted. 'I wouldn't go so far as to say that.'

'I think I'll go to his office. Or is he at Nearn House? I could do with a grape and I want to see him anyway to discuss the paint on Clarence's tail. And the photographs thereof.'

He came down off his high horse in a hurry, grabbed my elbow and hurried me out into the street. He wanted me to get into one of the panda cars, but I had no intention of being seen being bustled into a police car. I led him to my car and we sat down in privacy.

'You bastard,' he said furiously. 'You promised!'

'That was before you started gate-crashing my friends'

houses while they're abroad. But I shall keep my promise,' I said, 'if you'll just tell me what the hell's going on. I thought we'd agreed that Charlie was ninety-nine per cent exonerated.'

'We didn't agree anything of the sort. If you remember, I suggested that your friend might have killed Mr Ricketts and that he or somebody else could have given in to sudden temptation and removed the do-it-yourself cash-card kit.'

I thought hard. 'I don't see why that should call for a search of his house, and as a matter of such urgency. It could have waited until Charlie comes back.'

'If he comes back.'

'You may be right,' I said. 'When he hears that his house has been searched he may well head for the hills, if only because he's afraid of what may have been planted on him.'

I was beginning to get hot under the collar and I could feel DS Waller's glare scorching my left ear. 'And just how might he come to hear about it?' he asked me.

'He's bound to phone up again, to ask how Clarence is getting over his injury.'

'I could keep you incommunicado.'

'Not legally,' I pointed out. 'Not at all, for more than an hour or two, without having lawyers coming at you from every direction. Do you think that I would have come here without bothering to mention where I was going, and why, to my two partners and,' I said, beginning to embroider on the truth, 'Mr Kitts, and Angus Todd who I was supposed to be meeting—'

'All right,' he said. 'All *right*!'

'But,' I said, 'you tell me what and why and I'll promise not to let any cats out of bags. And I'll promise the same for anybody who I've already told. You'll have to deal with Charlie's neighbours yourselves. He could very well phone up to ask if his house is still standing. If he was guilty of anything, which I don't believe for a moment, he might do that anyway just to find out whether there had been any unusual activity.'

DS Waller grunted unhappily. 'Somehow, your promise isn't worth a lot just now,' he said.

'It's the best I've got to offer,' I pointed out.

'That isn't a hell of a comfort, but I suppose it'll have to do. All right, I'll explain a little more. But,' he said through clenched teeth, 'if you allow anybody to warn Mr Hopewell against coming home, I'll make a clean breast of it and have you charged with threatening an officer, interfering with the course of justice and anything else the Procurator-fiscal can dream up. On the other hand, if you breathe a word about my disclosures I'll get my Fife colleagues to fit you up for something so ridiculous and humiliating that you'll never dare to show your face at a field trial again.'

I was in no position to argue. 'Get on with it,' I said.

'On your head be it. Detective Chief Inspector McStraun had it figured that, whether your friend Mr Hopewell was a secret lover or an accomplice in the forging of bank cards, he was the one person who could have had a motive for cutting off his own dog's tail.'

Beth might have followed, but I was left behind. 'What motive?' I asked blankly.

'Once Clarence got that peculiar colour of paint on his tail, whether or not he had gone there with his master or made his own way on a food-seeking foray, he was a breathing, walking implication – if not proof positive – that Mr Hopewell was a visitor to Nearn House. And Clarence lived almost next door to a senior police officer.'

'That's slim grounds for breaking into a man's home during his absence,' I said.

'And the DCI was prepared to wait for Mr Hopewell's return. But then we had a tip-off that there was something significant to be found. It was decided to seek a warrant immediately, before he had time to vanish or – ' he looked at me with meaning ' – have a friend clear the place out. The friend who is getting so peevish because we beat him to it. And,' the Sergeant added indignantly, 'we didn't break in; we got the key from his neighbour.'

I decided to ignore the slur on myself. 'Tip-off from whom?'

'No,' said the DS firmly. 'At that point I must draw the line.'

'Tell me or the deal's off.'

'Remember what we've both got to lose. I've certainly got it in mind. My job's on the line here.'

'In other words, it was anonymous.' I was guessing, but he did not contradict me. 'So what did you find?' There was a long pause. 'Buy my silence,' I said.

He sighed. 'This is the absolute end,' he said. 'After this, nothing.' His cutting-off gesture was so violent that it made my car rattle.

'Agreed.'

'Remember, it's against my better judgement that I'm trusting you at all. We found another blank plastic card, identical to the first, in a dark corner of the hallway.'

'Was it—?'

'No. I told you. Nothing more.' His voice was deafening in the small space.

'For Christ's sake,' I said, 'I'm not asking for a state secret. All I wanted to know is whether it was in a position where it could have been flicked through the letter-box.'

'Well, it wasn't. We thought of that. And, anyway, there's a wire cage over the letter-box. And that is quite definitely your lot,' he said briskly. 'Go and drive yourself back across the Tay. Take the short route, don't bother to use the bridge.'

He got out of my car and slammed the door so hard that, when I reversed away from the police car in front, there was a rectangle of red dust beneath where the car had been.

The dashboard clock said that it was almost lunchtime. I could see Mrs Bell peeping out of her friend's front window. I made signs indicative of eating and drinking and she nodded violently. I drove round to the hotel.

The public phone was under a Perspex hood in the vesti-bule of the hotel, where the hungry and thirsty were

160

trickling by. I found a Phonecard with some credit left on it. Isobel answered the phone at Three Oaks. Every word that I said had a high chance of being heard by not less than three people, so I kept it brief and left a message for Beth. If by any chance Charlie phoned, no mention was to be made of my reason for coming to Foleyburn. In fact, it would be better if nothing whatever was said about the events of the past few days, just reassure him about Hannah and Clarence and ask what the weather was like in France. Isobel was intrigued but she gave me her word and promised to pass the message on.

I looked for Mrs Bell outside and then in the bar, but I had not seen her car in the car park and she would have had to sprint to arrive there so soon on foot.

The first familiar face that I saw belonged to Bob Roberts. He was nursing the remains of a pint at the bar counter and glowering at himself in the mirror behind the ranked bottles. I took the adjacent stool and invited him to have another pint. His beard seemed to register qualified approval. When our beers were poured and paid for, he moved to a table, jerking his head for me to follow.

'The police are searching your friend Hopewell's house, I'm told,' he said.

'Told by whom?'

'It's all over the village. Is that what brought you over?'

'I came to see if there was anything I could do.'

'And is there?'

'Not that I can see.'

He hummed tunelessly for a moment. 'From the questions the police was asking, they think Mr Hopewell was a brown-hatter. Queer. Know what I mean?'

'I know what you mean. What did you tell them?'

'Same as a'body else. He's no more queer than I am. And that's not at all,' he added fiercely. 'Losh, I hope I'm as vigorous when I'm his age.'

'He could just be putting on an act,' I suggested, more to test the water than because I had any doubts about Charlie's heterosexuality.

Roberts shook his head violently and his beard took on a sneer of its own. 'If it's an act, it's a bloody good one. It's got the women fooled.' He lowered his voice. 'He's not one to crow, I'll say that for him, but my wife does hairdressing in folk's own homes and she hears things. Since his wife died, your friend Charlie Hopewell hasn't gone out looking for his nooky, not quite, but he hasn't turned away from what's been on offer, not if it was clean and had most of its own teeth. And there's more than one unmarried lady, and the occasional widow, pleased enough to take up wi' an eligible widower wi' a nice house and not short of a bob or two, even if it'd mean taking on a lassie who's—' He met my eye and broke off. 'All right. I'll not say it aloud, but you ken fine what's adae there.'

'You can say it aloud,' I said. 'She's her own girl and she doesn't care who knows it.'

'Aye. That's one way of putting it. Another would be that she's wild. She's an angel the most of the time, but when that temper lets go . . . Whatever, I know for a fact that her dad's had that woman behind the bar. And she's not one to be free wi't.'

From what he was saying, Charlie had retained rather more vigour than I had been left with after my illness. I fought back a feeling of envy. 'I see,' I said. 'What else were the police asking?'

'Nothing out of the ordinary. Who had been seen around Nearn House or the cottages on the Friday and Saturday nearly three weeks back? When were your pal Hopewell or his lassie last seen out our way? When was Clarence seen, with or without his tail? And who was the regular visitor at Nearn House?'

So the pathologist had placed the death around the date when Clarence lost his tail. After such a delay and in weather which would not have encouraged the growth of insects, they would have had difficulty narrowing it down to even two days. If, however, they had discovered when and where he ate his last meal, they would have their answer to within an hour or two. More probably, they had found traces of drink or a bar meal in his stomach and his last visit to the hotel was remembered.

'Are they getting answers?' I asked.

'Not to the last one. There's not a soul will admit having been near the place, except yon van-driver and the postie. Not even the milkman.'

'He took UHT milk,' I said. 'Bought it in bulk.'

'So. If anybody's told them anything about anything worth a damn, nobody's told me.' Roberts looked slightly cheered by the thought.

Mrs Bell had arrived in the bar. She had settled at the corner table where we had sat more than a week earlier and she was wiggling her eyebrows at me. I asked Bob Roberts a few more questions without learning anything of use.

With an abrupt change of mood and subject he said, 'You was right.'

'I was?'

'Aye. I'm going offshore wi' the rest of them. Young Strachan fixed it for me. I'm not one to suck the public tit.'

'I'm glad,' I said. I declined a hesitant offer to buy me a drink in return and made my escape.

Mrs Bell had already ordered the tagliatelle, but she allowed me to fetch her her usual shandy. 'How did you get on?' she asked as I sat down.

'I couldn't do much. Nor could the solicitor,' I said. Remembering my promise I chose my words carefully. 'My guess is that they've had a tip, probably anonymous. Tell me, is there any likelihood that Charlie might phone you or your friend Mildred to ask whether everything was all right at home?'

'I shouldn't think so. But the police have already been round to utter terrible warnings about what we mustn't say if he should happen to phone. We had to give our solemn promises. That young Detective Sergeant was threatening to have our phones disconnected if we didn't.'

Mrs Bell spoke as though having her phone cut off would be the end of civilization as she knew it, which might well have been the case.

She had been sworn to secrecy, so there was no point in trying to keep her in the dark. If she broke her word, it would make little difference how much more she knew. I told her the rest of what I had been able to squeeze out of the Sergeant.

'But that's a whole load of nonsense,' she said when I had finished. 'For one thing, those houses were all built at the same time and they have the same baskets inside the letter-boxes. One day, I had a long thin box to put through Mildred's letter-box – she'd lent me her electric carving-knife and I knew that she was needing it back but she was out when I called. Well, to cut a long story slightly shorter, it was too long for the wire basket but I found that I could push the flap of the wire box up with a piece of stick and pop the other box through. Anybody could do the same and flick a plastic card inside.

'And I'll tell you something else. Charlie Hopewell wasn't the mysterious visitor. It's true that he goes out for walks with Clarence every day, but I've seen him when I've been at the shops. Sometimes he goes out past the cottages, but I've seen him just as often on the other road.'

'That isn't exactly conclusive,' I said, and I explained about the van.

'Well, there's another—' Mrs Bell bit off her words. 'Look who's here,' she said, without any sign of pleasure.

I looked round. Carol Haven – Mrs Postman Pat – was slipping between the tables. Her make-up was again perfect, but this time, instead of windblown hair and an inspired casualness of garb suitable for the garden, she wore an inexpensive dress which must have been chosen more for its flattering sheerness rather than for the warmth demanded by the weather. To my inexpert eye it looked very slightly dated. Her hair might have only just emerged from one of the great salons. Male eyes were covertly following her and she knew it; but outwardly as she reached our table she was only showing pleased recognition.

'Janet Bell!' she said brightly. 'And Mr Cunningham! I didn't know that you two knew each other. You don't mind if I come and play gooseberry?' Without giving Mrs Bell time to express her evident abhorrence of the idea, she took the chair opposite to mine and studied the menu. 'Isn't it awful about poor Charlie?'

'Isn't what in particular awful about Charlie?' Mrs Bell demanded.

Mrs Haven looked at her vaguely. 'Well, whatever it is, it can't be very good, can it? His house being searched and all that. There are rumours going around that he's been mixed up in something really bad. Worse, I mean, than just being queer.'

That was going too far. 'You really ought to watch what you're saying,' I said. 'Charlie only lost his wife a few years ago. And you told me yourself that he'd made passes at you and that he'd told you that it was your fault rather than his that you were born thirty years too late for him. I think that those were the words you quoted.'

'Thirty?' Mrs Bell's strong face registered amazement and we were left in no doubt that what had bedazed her was the size of the estimated gap between the ages of Charlie and Mrs Haven.

The latter looked hastily out of the window. 'Well, yes,' she said. 'But he'd have run a mile if I'd taken him up on it.' I met Mrs Bell's eye and she winked. Carol Haven, she was saying, was a scandalmonger who couldn't bear the thought of any man not being after her long-lost virtue, not even one whom she was at the same moment denouncing as homosexual. Mrs Haven was quick to see a second way out. 'And I didn't say for sure that he was that way inclined, I said that whatever trouble he was in was supposed to be worse.' So there! said her tone of voice.

The waitress brought my filled, baked potato. Mrs Haven snapped the menu shut. 'I'll have the chicken paella,' she said.

There was a pause. I gathered that I was expected to

offer her a drink. I asked the question and ordered a glass of the house white. The waitress went away.

'What I was about to say before ... what did you say your name was, dear?' Mrs Bell enquired pleasantly.

Mrs Haven flushed. 'I'm Carol Haven, as I think you know very well.'

'Put it down to my awful memory,' Mrs Bell said. She then went on to demonstrate that she had a perfectly sound memory for names. 'What I was going to tell Mr Cunningham was that there's another reason why Charlie Hopewell couldn't have been the regular visitor at Nearn House. It was late one afternoon, after dark, and I bumped into you outside the village shop talking to Jenny Laing. You have always been the one person who was most curious about whether Mr Ricketts was bent and the identity of his visitor—'

Carol Haven pouted her luscious, dark lips. 'Well, you must admit that it was intriguing, to wonder if it was one of the local husbands and whether his wife knew that he'd have preferred her to be a man. If he did,' she added.

Mrs Bell paused to wonder whether there were any points to score off that remark and decided against it. 'You said that you'd just been for a walk up the Foley Burn and you'd met a figure shrouded in a hat with a turned-down brim and a mac with a turned-up collar, who switched his torch off and hurried by. And I was just about to say that if you were so desperate to know all the answers you'd only have to note which of the local men didn't respond to your overtures, when Charlie Hopewell came out of the baker's next door, wearing an anorak and a flat cap, and you started telling him all about it. You never even noticed me slipping away.'

Carol Haven shrugged. 'I could have been wrong. That one time it could have been some other man walking along the burn.'

'Was he tall or short?' I asked. 'Fat or thin?'

'It was dark. He seemed about average.'

I was about to ask whether he walked with a limp,

smelled of aftershave, sounded asthmatic or had any other features recognizable in the near-darkness when we were interrupted. Beth came stalking through the bar and halted at our table. 'So this is where I find you!' she declaimed. 'Lunching with not one but two other women.'

Beth was serious, but not about my apparent infidelity. I sensed that she was rather enjoying playing a part. 'Mrs Bell,' I said without rising, 'and Mrs Haven. The lady talking through her hat is my wife, Beth.'

'How do you do, my dear?' Mrs Bell said cheerfully.

Jealous wives were no novelty to Carol Haven. 'We'll have to stop meeting like this,' she said in a husky voice, pitched just loudly enough to attract the attention of the nearby tables. She kissed the air a foot from my cheek, snorted with amusement, then got up and moved to another table, beckoning to the waitress who was approaching with her lunch.

'Simple but effective,' Mrs Bell said approvingly, modestly aware that no suspicion could possibly attach to herself.

'I thought it might do the trick,' Beth said. She then produced out of thin air what I still think of as the ultimate insult. Taking the seat just vacated by Mrs Haven she jumped to her feet again. 'Too hot,' she explained loudly and moved to the fourth chair. Mrs Bell was openly laughing and I heard suppressed snickers from nearby tables. Carol Haven, who had moved to a table already occupied by two interested men, looked daggers – but in silence.

Mrs Bell seemed to have taken an instant liking to Beth. 'It didn't take you long to get the measure of that little madam,' she said.

Beth pushed away the menu that I was offering her. 'I've eaten,' she said. 'No. John described her to me, so I knew what to expect. I didn't really mind him talking to her but I didn't think that she was the sort of person we'd want to discuss Charlie Hopewell's predicament with.'

'I'm glad my description was so adequate,' I said.

'It wasn't adequate at all,' Beth said sternly. 'You missed

out several important snippets of information. But it was enough. Now, please, between you, tell me everything that's going on. It's important.'

'Did you come all this way just for that?' I asked her. 'And, come to think of it, how did you get here?'

'I made Isobel bring me across, but she's gone back now so I'm dependent on you for a lift home. What did you expect? I get back from the village and Isobel gives me a most peculiar message from you, saying that if Charlie phones up we're to keep him in the dark. Does that mean that you think that he killed Mr Ricketts? And if so, why?'

'It doesn't mean anything of the sort,' I said. 'But the police are suspicious and your friend the Sergeant's head will be on the block if Charlie's forewarned.'

'But why do the police think that Charlie would do such a thing?'

Between us, we brought her up to date. Sometimes I found Beth's insistence on verbatim reporting tiresome, but there was no doubt that it clarified one's own recollections. The bar was closing by the time Beth had dragged out of us every word that everybody had said to anybody else right up to the moment of her arrival, but she made no comment except to remark that we had work to do back at the kennels. She thanked Mrs Bell. 'You're a real friend to Charlie,' she said. 'I can tell.'

Mrs Bell actually blushed. 'I hope so,' she said.

'We'll make sure that Charlie knows how much he owes you,' Beth assured her.

Beth was very silent for most of our trip home. I knew that to interrupt her and break her intensive train of thought was the one sure way to put her at odds with me, so I waited. I had stopped at the toll-gate and was pulling onto the bridge when she stirred and looked around.

'What did you mean by your last remark?' I asked her.

'What remark?' Beth asked vaguely. 'Oh, I remember. She's in love with Charlie.'

It had never occurred to me that love could come to the over-forties. 'Surely not!' I said.

168

'There's no doubt of it. You could hear her voice change every time she mentioned his name. And he's too busy flirting with every woman he meets to notice any one of them in particular. Well, he's getting too old for that sort of life. We'll just have to give him a little push. They'd be very good for each other. He'll need somebody like her when he doesn't have Hannah any more.'

It always amazes me how Beth can attune to the least suggestion of a romance. She is seldom wrong. 'I didn't notice anything,' I said.

'You wouldn't.'

'Probably not,' I said. 'What was it that I didn't tell you about Carol Haven?'

'Several things.'

I was stung. 'Name one,' I said.

'The colour of her nail varnish,' Beth said after a moment's thought.

'Very funny!' I said cuttingly.

Beth was thoughtful and rather curt for the rest of the day, and I sensed that she was worried. I knew that she used the telephone more than once but, as she had said, we had work to do. Isobel was away, taking one of our brood bitches for the service of the chosen stud dog, and she had taken Hannah along, at the latter's own request and for the furtherance of her education. It was only after the work was done that Beth seemed ready to talk. Sam was in his playpen in the corner of the kitchen and I was teasing him with a ball on a string while Beth prepared our dinner.

We had only said a few words when the phone rang. Beth jumped to answer it.

'Remember,' I said, 'if it's Charlie, not a word.'

The call was from a possible client. Beth made an appointment for two days ahead and went back to the stove. 'I don't see why I should feel bound by your promises,' she said in a very small voice. 'I have the right to make my own decisions.'

'I always consult you if I can,' I said. 'In this instance,

I had no alternative. I had to promise first and consult you afterwards. Was that so awful?'

'Suppose I didn't agree with you? I don't believe in secrets.'

That was true. Beth was the most open person that I had ever met. I sought for words to put the thing into perspective. 'If Charlie's innocent,' I said, 'as we both believe, warning him wouldn't change anything. He'd still have to come home and face the music. All you'd do would be to worry him and maybe cause him to have a traffic accident, and also get Detective Sergeant Waller into deep trouble with his boss after he's been open with us and we've pressured him into stepping over the line. If by any chance Charlie's guilty, he can't cut and run. The French police are probably tracking him already.'

'That may be so,' Beth said. 'I just don't like the feeling that somebody else, even you, can make promises for me. You feel the same. That's why we don't have a joint account.'

'The reason that we don't have a joint account is because we're both nervous that we might each be writing cheques on it at the same moment. If you ever feel the need to make promises in my name, go right ahead. I'll agree to be bound by them. I may take a whippy stick to you afterwards if I don't agree with you, but I'll honour your promise at the time. Shall I take Sam up and start his bath?'

'Please.'

I carried the sleepily protesting Sam upstairs, stripped him off and dunked him in warm water. I was giving him a rinse and a tickle when Beth came to join us.

'Don't wake him up too much,' she said. She took Sam from me and wrapped him in a warm towel. 'What's Charlie going to think if he phones up and we don't say a word, and he turns up at home in the middle of a huge row and a police inquisition?'

'We can explain,' I said. 'He'll understand.'

'He'd better. I'll leave you to do the explaining.'

'You usually do,' I said. 'You do realize that if Charlie,

170

innocent or guilty, goes to jail, we may be stuck with Hannah?'

'It won't happen. But would you hate it?' Beth asked me.

I jumped at the chance of a change of subject. 'Not if you wouldn't,' I said. 'She's good with the dogs and a hard worker. With no O levels and a reputation for rebelliousness, it could be the only job that will be open to her.'

'So if we take her on, we probably have her for good?'

'Not necessarily. If we teach her the business, when Charlie pops his clogs she may set up on her own.'

Beth nodded solemnly. 'Long before then, we should know if she's going to work out all right. I think she will. She's happy here and there's nobody she's in the habit of resenting to order her around, so I've been bossing her about without even getting a dirty look. All right. We'll speak to Charlie. It's a joint decision.'

'What about Isobel?'

'She suggested it. Remember,' Beth said, 'it's a joint decision. I'm not committing you without you knowing it.'

After that, it was inevitable that the phone should be busy off and on all evening. Friends, clients, suppliers, all seemed anxious for a few words. At every ring, the tension struck an arc between us again. Hannah, dropped off with the bitch by Isobel, reported that the service had proceeded to the satisfaction of all parties and then, sensing stress in the air, hurried off to bed.

The last call came just as we were preparing to go upstairs. I was already on the way up. Beth took the call in the kitchen. I heard her say Charlie's name and I came down quickly.

'Clarence is all right,' Beth was saying. 'His wound healed well and he's getting his confidence back. And Hannah has been staying here.' There was a pause while the receiver quacked into her ear. 'No, she's really been very good indeed. She's a natural with the dogs. We could certainly offer her a job here on a trial basis if you thought . . . We couldn't promise that it would lead to a career – how could we? – but at least it would be what they call Work Experience. She could stay here most of the week and go to you whenever she takes days off . . . How's the weather wherever you are?'

When she hung up, I was waiting in the doorway. 'They're nearing Boulogne,' she said. 'They'll cross tomorrow and be with us, probably, early the next day. And he's over the moon at the idea that Hannah might have a job with us. I think he'd resigned himself to having her on his hands indefinitely.'

We climbed the stairs together. 'It didn't hurt all that much, now, did it?' I asked her.

'I knew all along that I'd have to honour your promise,' she said. 'But you may care to remember that I gave the Sergeant a promise in both our names about the photographs, when he came to see us the day before yesterday, and you don't seem to have felt very bound by it. So I was just going after you with that whippy stick of yours.'

I laughed but she was looking serious. She looked first to see that Sam was sleeping peacefully and then followed me into the bedroom. 'You'd better make yourself clean and tidy in the morning. I phoned Detective Chief Inspector McStraun and we're going to go and see him at Nearn House at midday tomorrow. That was the earliest that he could spare the time. I must see him before Charlie gets home.'

My first thought was for DS Waller. 'You're not going to dump that poor young man in it, are you?' I asked.

'I don't think so. I . . . I don't want to talk about it, if you don't mind. I'm not sure of anything and I'm scared of being wrong. Please, John?'

A period of intricate debate would only have brought on my insomnia. 'You can tell me whenever you feel ready.'

'Thank you. I quite like you, sometimes,' she said.

TEN

We never did keep our appointment with Detective Chief Inspector McStraun.

I slept badly that night. I was aware of Beth's restlessness and knew that, having once again assumed responsibility for everybody's ills, she was turning things over and over in her mind, checking and re-checking in readiness for her encounter with the Detective Chief Inspector and in her very genuine fear of committing what to her was the ultimate sin – being wrong and letting Charlie and me and Hannah down. And she would not let me help. She had said once that she thought better on her own. Perhaps her thought processes were different – as if her computer program was in another language.

Breakfast was only a memory and Sam was twanging around the kitchen in his Baby Bouncer, when a police Range Rover arrived bearing Detective Sergeant Waller. Beth and Hannah were making up the meals for the puppies, while Isobel and I attended to cleaning the runs and grass, irritably telling each other that partners shouldn't have to do that kind of dirty work and that even if Hannah came to us on a regular basis a second kennel-maid would not be out of the question, provided that we could get one out of the Work Experience programme.

The Sergeant seemed to be dazed. We had parted in anger but he seemed to bear me no ill will. My first thought was to put him to work on run-cleaning until he had pulled himself together, but Beth had other ideas.

She handed over the feeding of the pups to Hannah, and took the Sergeant into the sitting room. As an afterthought, she invited me to follow. The runs, it seemed, could wait. I gave Isobel an apologetic shrug, trying to convey in that one movement my absolute incomprehension as to what was going on and a promise to relay the information to her, in full detail and glorious Technicolor, as soon as I had it myself.

The room was not cold, but Beth had put a match to the fire. She had also found time to do something clever with her hair. The Sergeant, whether he knew it or not, was highly privileged. Beth joined me on the couch. The making of a fire was a reflex gesture conveying hospitality and comfort and, I thought, by satisfying Beth's own nest-building instinct, it gave her reassurance about her place in the circle. The magical flick to the hair was a signal that work was suspended and that she wanted to please. Ritual satisfied, we were in a familiar pattern, ready to talk.

'How on earth did you do it?' the Sergeant enquired respectfully of Beth.

'Do what?' I asked, much less respectfully. Beth hates to speak out until she is quite sure of her ground. But I had had more than enough of trying to operate in the dark during my army days. And my anxiety on Charlie's behalf was coming to a head.

Detective Sergeant Waller turned to me as if in explanation. 'Mrs Cunningham phoned the Detective Chief Inspector yesterday afternoon. I don't know what she said – I was listening so intently for any sign that you'd dropped me in it that I missed half of the half I could hear. But he got onto the lab straight away and told them to make another and closer examination of the severed tail. I don't know any more detail than that – I only caught the tail-end of the call, if you'll forgive the pun – but I could tell that the lab put up an argument, making out that they hate to risk interfering with evidence unnecessarily, but my guess is that they don't much like being told how to do their jobs by non-scientific officers.

'We had no time for discussion, even if he'd felt like telling me more, because the pathologist's full report came in at long last, with apologies for delays caused by a severe shortage of typists. The Chief went through it, reading out to me any bits which he deemed to be significant, until he came to a bit of the real nitty gritty. It seems that the unfortunate Mr Ricketts had been impotent from birth. There were indications that at some time in the distant past he might have accepted the role of a passive sodomite, but that would have been to suit his own interests. His heart would not have been in it.'

Beth brushed aside the Detective Sergeant's euphemisms. 'You mean that he wouldn't have got any pleasure out of it?'

'Er, yes. I was still with the Detective Chief Inspector when the lab called back, sounding excited.

' "By God!" says the Chief, "it all makes sense now," and he starts shooting out orders like a Roman candle. The lab was to finish cleaning up the unburnt part of the table-top and check the kitchen floor under the bloodstains while he went for a search warrant. I nearly gave three cheers, because it meant that you'd kept your word and that I was off the hook.'

Satisfied that he had given me all the explanation that I needed, the Sergeant turned back to Beth. 'We went to serve the warrant just before midnight,' he said. 'Unfortunately, something must have tipped them off and the birds had flown. Those sort of people have sensitive antennae and it's easy for an officer to give something away. But, sure enough, we found the card-copying machine and a whole lot of blank cards identical to the one from Ricketts's table. They must have known that once Postman Pat deserted his – er – post there would be no more cards to copy.

'Information's still coming in, but already we've learned a lot. His car turned up at Glasgow Airport and we're almost sure which flight they were on but not what names and passports they're using. Other forces have been alerted. If they ever start drawing money on those cards they'll be nailed. Even if they've gone somewhere where they're safe from extradition they will still have committed an offence, and before you know it they'll spill the beans, each trying to put as much of the blame as possible onto the other. It happens nine times out of ten.'

Once her immediate worry was over, Beth's concern was again for others. 'You won't have had much sleep,' she said.

The Sergeant, now that he had been reminded of sleep, fought back a yawn. 'About two hours,' he said. 'But I'll catch up tonight. First thing this morning, the Detective Chief Inspector sent me to convey his warmest thanks and congratulations while updating your statements. He would also be deeply grateful – we both would – if you would tell us what put you onto it in the first place.'

'Did he really say all that?' Beth asked delightedly.

'In so many words?' I added.

'Well, not in those exact words, perhaps. What he actually said, as near as I can remember, was "Get over there, thank her for the helpful suggestion and ask her what tipped her off." '

'I see.' Beth, who is not proud, flashed me a grin. Before speaking out she paused and listened, but the rhythmic sound of Sam on his Baby Bouncer was the sound of a thoroughly entranced infant. Suspended in a sort of miniature bosun's chair by rubber shock-cord, he needed only to push himself off from the floor to rise or swing; and he had brought the art to a standard suitable for an Olympic event.

'Presumably,' I said, 'you intend to do a little editing. To save the DCI's face and your neck.'

'Well, yes,' Waller admitted.

'All right,' Beth said. 'So what you really need is a clue which I had and you didn't.'

'Boy, do I ever,' said the DS. 'Pretty please,' he added with feeling. 'If you can think of one.'

Beth cast up her eyes and thought for a minute and another grin spread over her face. 'Here you are, then,' she said. She was watching me out of the corner of her eye. 'The moment I saw the colour of Mrs Haven's nail varnish I was sure that I was right. When Mr McStraun showed us the photograph of the severed tail, I noticed that the tip seemed to be much the colour of the liver part of Clarence's coat as well as looking sort of matted.

'I remembered what you said, John. Clarence refused to get out of the car at the bodywork shop. The smell of cellulose reminded him of the smell of nail varnish. So I looked back through some old snapshots until I found some with Clarence in them, and although photographs of dogs aren't usually taken from behind they did seem to confirm what I remembered, that Clarence's tail had had a white tip. That's the bit that you can tell your Mr McStraun. And it seemed in turn to confirm what I'd been having vague thoughts about all along, because she'd said that she heard Clarence screeching when he came home, but what Mrs Bell told John suggested that her car had been going out past the cottages not much earlier.

'What I think had been making everybody boggle at the edges, if that's the phrase I want, was two extraordinary sort of things happening in the same place and around the same time – a murder and a tail-chopping. But here we had an explanation for the two things rolled together, which made them much easier to swallow.'

The Sergeant was nodding happily, like one of those dogs in the back windows of cars, but they had left me far behind. 'I don't understand,' I said.

'No, of course you don't,' Beth said comfortingly. 'I'll explain. The Sergeant told us about the faked bank cards. Not credit cards, mind, which would require copies that looked just like the original.'

'Because shop assistants handle them,' I said, to show that I was still awake and not as far behind as all that.

'Yes. A bank card works in the machine and nobody need see it at all if you're careful, but – and here's the big point – you have to have a Personal Identity Number that matches the card. And they make an awful fuss about keeping that number a closely guarded secret. Some people do write the number down in some hidden place and in a disguised sort of way, in case they forget it, and I expect that a clever pickpocket can often find or figure out the number. But these people weren't picking pockets or snatching handbags, they were copying bank cards.'

'Exactly,' said Detective Sergeant Waller. 'And although there have been one or two very rare instances of a high-tech criminal managing to hack into a bank's computer and collect PIN numbers, that information's so heavily protected that it is very rare indeed, and when it happens it gets detected. With Jason Ricketts on our doorstep, and in view of his record, we wondered whether he hadn't reached that or an even higher degree of sophistication, but he seldom left home except to get tanked up in the hotel, where he spoke to nobody in particular, and he didn't have access to a computer.'

'He could have had a personal computer and worked over the telephone,' I said. 'Or did you search the place?'

'Nearn House didn't have a telephone,' said the DS. 'Owing to a lack of lines, Telecom couldn't give him a phone until the week before he died. So that knocked that idea on the head. Ricketts's possible or even probable involvement was discussed endlessly; but I'll remind you that the case was at an early stage and we had other and bigger cases to wind up.'

Beth cleared her throat modestly as if to remind us that she had not finished answering the question. We waited. 'It seemed to me,' she said, 'that the other weak point was that both the cards and the PIN numbers are sent through the post. A dishonest postman could get access to them.

'And there was a postman nearby who had more money than you'd expect of a humble postie.'

'Postman Pat!' I exclaimed.

'Right,' said the Sergeant. 'And what none of us knew

was that he already had a criminal record. He seems to have furnished a convincing if fraudulent background when applying for the job – probably furnished by Ricketts – and we only got onto him just before Ricketts died. As a postman, he did deliveries in one of the best areas of Dundee. He could easily hold back likely looking mail for a day or two. The way the mails have been, who'd notice? And it's quite possible to guess whether what's inside is worth taking a closer look at.'

'I'm told that you can buy a solution for the purpose,' I said.

The Sergeant hesitated. 'Don't you go spreading this around, but common methylated spirit makes most papers go transparent for long enough for somebody to study the interior of an envelope,' he said reluctantly. 'And it leaves very little trace behind when it dries. Even the smell soon fades away. But confidential bank correspondence travels in envelopes which transfer coloured dye to the contents if any such trick has been used. Haven's previous convictions were for theft. He was unlikely to know how to open and close an envelope without giving himself away and he certainly couldn't copy a bank card.

'The coincidence of a postman, with a criminal record, delivering in the areas in which lived most of the account-holders who had complained of the disputed withdrawals, was enough to make us sit up. Not far away from him lived another convicted felon, a high-tech villain who would be perfectly capable of doing all the rest. But, there was no sign that they even knew each other. In fact, we've since discovered that they were in Peterhead Prison at the same time, but that's all, and we didn't find that much out until two days ago.

'Quite by chance, Postman Pat had come to live next door to Detective Chief Inspector McStraun. Just what the postman's thoughts were when he first found out who his new neighbour was is a matter of guesswork; but he must soon have decided to turn it to his advantage. Mr McStraun, aided by his observant wife, was in a perfect position to swear that Haven went off to his work every day like a good little postman, returned at the end of his shift and rarely went out again. Most of his leisure was spent working in his garden and joining with Mr McStraun in complaining about the ravages of Clarence. On that subject, at least, they were on the same side.

'Meanwhile, Mrs Haven was in the habit of going out several times a week, sometimes walking and sometimes driving. She had a bright yellow Metro which was unmistakable and has never been seen nearer to Nearn House than sweeping past the end of the drive. We now guess that she would pick up the van from its hiding-place, put on the hat and gloves and mackintosh which were left inside it and drive to Nearn House. There, she would wait while Ricketts made his copies and resealed the envelopes. She was very careful, judging from the scarcity of the traces she left behind, but her waiting around might easily extend to an hour or more. The one relaxation she allowed herself from her self-imposed standards of caution must have been to remove her gloves at the kitchen table and do her nails. The kitchen table was also where Ricketts worked, for the sake of the light and the availability of power and water nearby, so she would have been able to observe over and over again how he performed his magic.'

The Sergeant was warming to his narrative. I would have enjoyed a cup of tea or coffee to go with it but I had no intention of interrupting the flow nor of missing a single word. I got up and helped myself to a beer and put another within the Sergeant's reach. Beth shook her head at me but the Sergeant did not seem to notice.

'There came the day,' he said, 'when their peaceful scene was rudely interrupted. We can date it accurately. The butcher's van had called and Ricketts had bought a small shoulder of lamb. Mr McCulloch remembers making the sale and that the small van was there at the time. The lamb must have been left sitting on the worktop. We found a matching bone among the trees.

'Ricketts had painted the outside door that morning but, because of the threat of rain, he had left it standing ajar so that it was sheltered by being inside the building. Clarence, exploring or drawn by the smell of meat, found his way inside, brushing the wet paint with his tail.'

'He used to be such a friendly dog,' Beth said sadly, 'and he liked people. Even when he was marauding he could never resist rushing at them to express his affection. I don't know that he'll ever do that again.'

'Perhaps not,' said the Sergeant. 'In his ebullience he must have arrived like a whirlwind, crashing against the kitchen table, knocking the nail varnish to the floor and in the process getting some on the tip of his tail. Traces were found on the table-top and the floor when the lab got around to cleaning off the last of the blood.

'At this point, Ricketts seems to have lost his head. By coincidence, the outermost half of Clarence's tail now carried two distinct contact traces, one of Nearn House and the other of Mrs Haven, and if not knocked on the head he would be returning to his home next door to DCI McStraun.'

'Not really such a coincidence,' Beth said. 'A happy dog's tail thrashes around. If anything's going to knock into things or get marked, it's the tail.'

The Sergeant absorbed this argument without losing his thread. 'It's very unlikely, in fact, that anybody would ever have noticed that the tip of Clarence's tail had changed colour to match Mrs Haven's rather unusual nail varnish. After all, that nail varnish was a good match for the liver colour of much of Clarence's coat, and there was nothing to show that the paint and the nail varnish had been acquired at the same time and place. If Ricketts had repainted his own door a different colour, nobody would ever have known or thought anything, and even the door would have been better for it. But ... what's that phrase in the Bible?'

' "The wicked flee when no man pursueth",' said Beth, who was well brought up. 'Is that what you meant?'

181

'That's just what I meant. Ricketts was an unstable character anyway, and in the heat of the moment Clarence's tail looked like a damning accusation pointed in his direction. It would be easier to hide the tail than a whole body, so he grabbed up his cleaver and lopped off the evidence, burying it later in the garden.'

'Alas, poor Clarence,' I said.

DS Waller nodded without bothering to comprehend. He noticed the beer in his hand for the first time and took a long pull. 'At this point,' he said, 'the statement by Mrs Turner, Mrs Bell's friend, becomes relevant. She saw Mrs Haven returning home after the rain and thought that she looked upset. This was enough to make her keep an eye on the Havens' house and she is certain that when Postman Pat arrived home his wife was waiting at the door in an agitated state and was pouring out some story before the door was properly shut.

'The Havens must have had a conference that night. They had already collected a large number of duplicated cards together with their associated PIN numbers, ready for a *coup*, and Mrs Haven must have been confident that she could take over Ricketts's role in the operation. Ricketts, on the other hand, was becoming a liability. We think that the trial runs with the fake cards which had alerted us were down to him – he was running out of money and he didn't want to wait any longer.'

'Also,' I said, remembering the lecturer's story, 'he had come a cropper once before by trying for the one big *coup* instead of settling for a steady trickle of modest returns.'

'The Havens, on the other hand,' said the Sergeant, 'would have looked on it as a long-term opportunity for the big *coup*, to be followed by retirement in some sunnier climate – not a chance to be rushed at. It also seems possible that they never had intended him to share in the proceeds.

'We may never be quite sure who did the deed. But from the evidence of Postman Pat's time-cards it seems likely that the female of the species ... and so on,' said the Sergeant, who seemed less than happy in the world of quotations. 'Whatever, within the next day or two – the pathologist can't be too precise – there was another card to copy and one of them took it to Ricketts. As soon as Ricketts had settled to work, he was chopped with his own cleaver. The machine, plus as many blank cards as possible, were removed in the freezer-bags which we found, heavily bloodstained, in the Havens' dustbin. But there was one card lost under the puddle of blood and also the tell-tale stain of the nail varnish, so they returned together after dark, carried the table outside and started the unsuccessful bonfire.'

'Wicked!' Beth said under her breath. As she saw the Sergeant to the door, I was left to wonder whether she was referring to the murder or to the docking of Clarence.

The Range Rover had only got as far as the gates when Beth was calling for Hannah. There was a pause while the girl washed her hands – an inflexible precautionary house rule after handling dogs – and then she joined us in the sitting room, smiling her serene smile, and sat down where Beth indicated.

Beth chose her words carefully. 'Hannah,' she said, 'you know that it's wrong to listen to other people's phone calls?'

Hannah's face froze. She nodded and looked away.

'When I phoned the Detective Chief Inspector yesterday,' Beth said, 'I thought that I could hear somebody walking on gravel. At the time I thought that the sound was coming from the end of the line, but now I think that you were listening outside on the cordless telephone. Why did you do it?'

Hannah took on a taut-faced, slit-eyed look which I recognized. I had seen it on Angus's face just before an explosion of temper. 'We're just considering offering you a steady job here,' I said gently. 'But if you ever lose your temper, you'll have to go. So learn to stay calm, and remember, any time that we ask you a question it's because we want to know the answer, not because we're

183

necessarily getting at you. So we'll ask you once more. Why?'

Hannah took several deep breaths and then nodded. I felt myself relax. I had been preparing for a clash and a confrontation. But now the tension melted away, leaving a warmth behind. Hannah would do.

She was looking at Beth. 'I heard you say something about my dad. I wanted to know what you were telling the police about him.'

'I see,' Beth said. 'But after that, you made a call, didn't you? I thought that I heard it clicking, but then I thought that I must be mistaken. There'll be a record of the call on our itemized phone bill,' she added when the girl hesitated.

Hannah nodded. 'Please,' she said, 'don't send me away.'

'You phoned Mrs Haven, didn't you?'

'Dad made me learn her number and Mrs Turner's in case I needed to phone home some time and he wasn't in,' Hannah said.

'You heard me tell Mr McStraun that he should search the Havens' house? What did I say that gave you the idea that they had killed Mr Ricketts?'

'Nothing,' said Hannah. 'But I already knew that.'

Beth frowned at me before I could speak. She paused and listened, but Sam was still swinging happily around. In addition, he was singing to himself. 'You'd better tell us the truth,' she said gently.

'I don't tell lies,' Hannah said firmly. She thought for several seconds and then nodded again. 'It was the day after Clarence's tail was cut. We'd fetched him home from the vet and that evening Dad decided that Clarence must go out to his kennel, same as usual. But I thought that Clarence would still be upset and afraid so I stayed outside and sat with him.

'It was dark and very quiet but quite warm. Mr and Mrs Haven forgot that their window was open, or else they didn't expect anybody to be outside in the dark.

Their kitchen window isn't far from Clarence's kennel. But I didn't mean to listen. Really I didn't.' Her eyes brimmed with tears.

'Of course you didn't,' Beth said. She moved to sit beside Hannah and put an arm round her. I realized suddenly that for all her adult rebelliousness, Hannah was still very young.

'You won't send me away?'

'Not if you keep your temper from now on,' I said, 'and tell the rest of it.'

'I heard Mrs Haven say that somebody was grouchy. So I listened because I thought that they might be speaking about me. It's the sort of thing they say.'

'Well, we don't say anything like that here,' Beth said. 'What were they saying?'

'Mr Haven said that there was no doubt about it, Mr Ricketts was going off his trolley – look what he'd done to that poor bloody spaniel. "We're going to have to deal with him." Those were his very words. They really were,' Hannah added anxiously.

'Of course they were,' Beth said. 'But, Hannah, why didn't you tell anybody all this?'

'I'd already asked Dad what we were going to do about the person who'd cut off Clarence's tail and he shook his head and said that there was nothing to be done. He said that revenge wouldn't do Clarence any good and that the best thing we could do would be to keep our heads down and wait and see; but that if he ever found out who it was he'd fix them good and proper.

'I knew that he was angry. I didn't want to make it worse and I was afraid that Dad might take some action and get into real trouble. So if Mr Ricketts had done that to Clarence and somebody else was going to do something to Mr Ricketts it seemed best not to say anything at all. And then – ' she looked at me ' – later, when you said that you were going to try to find out things, you said that we'd all have to be careful and not say too much.'

'I believe I did.'

185

Hannah nodded emphatically. 'Nobody told me that Mr Ricketts was dead until I heard you on the phone. Then I guessed what had happened. Perhaps it was right that Mr and Mrs Haven should be punished for killing the man who cut off Clarence's tail but, privately, I rather hoped that they'd get away with it. It seemed to me that he had to be the sort of person who was better dead.'

'So you phoned up and warned them,' Beth said. We sat for a minute in silence broken only by the crackle of the fire, the crunch of Isobel's feet on the gravel outside and the sounds of Sam in his bouncer, 'You were right,' Beth said. 'Best not to say anything at all. Can you manage that? Say nothing at all about what you heard and did? Not even to your dad?'

Hannah nodded happily. 'It would only worry him,' she said. 'Can I go now? Mrs Kitts wanted me to help her.'

Charlie phoned that evening. 'We've stopped off near Glasgow,' he said. 'We should be nearing home before lunchtime tomorrow. May we stop in and collect Hannah and Clarence?'

'That'll be all right,' I said.

'How is the old devil?'

'Getting back on form. Beth had him out this morning and he knocked over the postman.'

'That sounds like him. And Hannah?'

'Doing well. We're ready to give her a job, if you approve.'

'That's good. We'll talk about it. Anything happened while I've been away?'

'Quite a lot,' I said. 'It seems that the reason why Clarence's tail was cut off was to cover up evidence in a murder case. The murder was committed by one of your neighbours.'

'Pull the other one,' Charlie said. 'Never mind. I'll see you in the morning and you can give me any real news then.'

He hung up.